SONGS IN THE
KEY OF
DEATH

Library and Archives Canada Cataloguing in Publication

Bankier, William
[Short stories. Selections]
    Songs in the key of death / William Bankier.

(Dime crime)
Some stories were previously published.
Issued in print and electronic formats.
ISBN 978-1-77161-073-5 (pbk.).--ISBN 978-1-77161-074-2 (html).--
ISBN 978-1-77161-075-9 (pdf)

    I. Title.

PS8553.A56A6 2014   C813'.54   C2014-906155-2
                                             C2014-906156-0

Pubished by Mosaic Press, Oakville, Ontario, Canada, 2014.
Distributed in the United States by Bookmasters (www.bookmasters.com).
Distributed in the U.K. by Gazelle Book Services (www.gazellebookservices.co.uk).

MOSAIC PRESS, Publishers
Copyright © 2014 the estate of William Bankier

Printed and Bound in Canada.
ISBN Paperback 978-1-77161-073-5
           ePub 978-1-77161-074-2
           ePDF 978-1-77161-075-9

Designed by Eric Normann

We acknowledge the financial support
of the Government of Canada through
the Canada Book Fund (CBF) for
this project.

Nous reconnaissons l'aide financière
du gouvernement du Canada par l'en-
tremise du Fonds du livre du Canada
(FLC) pour ce projet.

 Canadian   Patrimoine
            Heritage   canadien

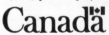

MOSAIC PRESS
1252 Speers Road, Units 1 & 2
Oakville, Ontario L6L 5N9
phone: (905) 825-2130

info@mosaic-press.com

www.mosaic-press.com

VOLUME 2

SONGS IN THE KEY OF

DEATH

WILLIAM BANKIER

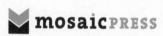

Contents

Songs in the Key of Death

The Fiction of William Bankier

by Peter Sellers

A MAN HEARS A WOMAN OPERATOR'S VOICE ON THE phone and, attracted and intrigued, he makes an appointment to meet her. Three questions spring to mind. What drives a man to ask? What kind of woman responds? And what godawful things are going to happen?

That basic premise, from William Bankier's story "Her Voice On The Phone Was Magic", is typical of his work. Acts committed on whim or on the basis of incomplete or incorrect information lead, invariably, to nightmare. But the characters involved aren't often given the blessed relief of waking up. At least, not in time. Also typical of Bankier, and evident in that outline, is the recurring theme of relationships as destructive and a breeding ground for all manner of evil.

Bankier himself is no stranger to acting on a whim. In 1974, having grown as he describes, "incurably dissatisfied with life as it stood", Bankier and his wife Phyllis packed up their two daughters, packed in his career in advertising, and headed for London where he was to live for ten years, much of it on a cramped houseboat moored on the Thames. Bankier left England after Phyllis' untimely death. He now lives in West Hollywood with his second wife, editor and gag-writer Felice Nelson. His daughters, Heather and Amy, continue to live and work in London.

Prior to his move, Bankier had published sporadically. He sold his first story to *Liberty Magazine* in 1954. A few years later, two horror stories appeared in the *Magazine of Fantasy* and *Science Fiction*. Then in 1962, *Ellery Queen Mystery Magazine* published "What Happened in Act One", Bankier's first professional crime fiction sale. Over the next ten years, he sold seven or eight more crime stories to the major mystery magazines. But once he left the advertising business in which he'd laboured for 25 years and became a full time writer, the floodgates opened. There were over 45 romantic "nurse" novelettes under a variety of women's names, and a steady stream of increasingly assured crime fiction.

That assurance has been reflected in Bankier's status as one of the most frequent contributors to *Ellery Queen Mystery Magazine* over the past two decades; an Edgar Award nomination in 1980; three Crime Writers of Canada Arthur Ellis Award nominations, and the 1992 CWC Derrick Murdoch Award for his lifetime of achievement.

Bankier started writing crime stories as a child in his native Belleville, Ontario. "A brother and I used to write a story together often on a Sunday afternoon, one writing a paragraph, the other coming along and reading it and adding the next paragraph. We killed off each other's characters and left the plot in impossible situations."

Decades later and three thousand miles away in LA, the killings continue. And characters are still thrust into impossible situations.

In Bankier's world, families aren't just unhealthy, they're dangerous. He doesn't always restrict himself to dysfunctional relationships between husbands and wives, or parents and children. Siblings, as in the deeply unsettling "The Prize In The Pack", included here, or the wonderfully titled "How Dangerous is Your Brother?", have their moments, too.

Titles and first lines are a Bankier strength. Richly evocative, the names of his stories often hint strongly at his underlying themes. "Girls, Like White Birds", "By the Neck Until Dead", "Only If You Get Caught". And the opening lines ("Darius Dolan climbed the iron stairs with another beer for his wife's lover") reinforce the menace and the message. Relationships don't work. Happiness is not a realistic goal. Shocking violence appears when you least expect it.

Despite the violent death in many of Bankier's stories, his work is not about bloodshed. His concern is motivation. What drives people to the actions they ultimately take? In stories such as "What Really Happened?" he goes so far as to apply that concern to real life, offering his solution to one of history's most fascinating murders, the Lizzie Borden case.

Although he played detective himself in that case (as well as later in "Death of a Noverint", about the killing of playwright Christopher Marlowe) Bankier has written about detectives only infrequently. Bankier's sole entry into the detective pantheon is Professor Harry Lawson, known as the "Praw", a former professional stage magician who specializes in finding people and objects that have disappeared. He, along with his voluptuous wife Lola and her slightly thick brother Al, made his first appearance in "The Mystery of the Missing Penelope" in December 1978. "The Mystery of the Missing Guy", followed the next year. However, after his third case, "The Missing Missile" in February, 1980, Praw Lawson himself disappeared without a trace. Lawson could possibly have stepped into the guild of detective magicians peopled by the likes of Clayton Rawson's Great Merlini, but whodunits are neither Bankier's interest nor his forte. They lie elsewhere: in Baytown, in sports, and in music.

In the geography of longitude and latitude, Baytown lies on the north shore of the St. Lawrence River, a little less than halfway along the main highway between Toronto and Montreal. In the inner geography of the soul, however, it lies about equidistant between despair and tragedy.

The people of Baytown are Bankier's true recurring characters. People who drift in and out of the ongoing series, changing, aging, gaining a promotion or losing their hair, giving the series a ring of truth beyond the emotional, forming a consistent backdrop for the action, occasionally stepping to centre stage. Radio station personality Clement Foy. Sammy Luftspring, the bellboy at the Coronet Hotel. Police chief Don Cleary. Coronet owner Jack Danforth.

In the Baytown stories, Bankier explores all his recurring themes. And the presence of Baytown colours most of his other fiction as well. A story may take place in Montreal or London or Los Angeles, but chances are at least one of the characters will be from Baytown. Creating unhappiness seems to be the towns' largest industry; killers its biggest export.

Many of those characters, whether at home or abroad in the Baytown diaspora, are performers and the action is centered around the arenas in which they perform. Invariably, the arenas are ones in which Bankier himself has held a long and active interest. Amateur theatrics, in which he has been a keen participant, are the basis for this collection's "The Last Act Was Deadly" but also show up in other tales such as "Rock's Last Role" and "Is There A Killer in the House?"

Bankier is an avid sports fan. "A sports watcher," he says, "not much of a doer." His particular passion is for baseball, a common theme most notably in the loosely connected Jonathan "Johnny Fist" Fitzwilliam stories. Other sports that come up include boxing in "The Dreams of Hopeless White" where a security guard's vision of a career in the ring ends in tragedy. Bankier's Canadian roots show in his use of hockey in "The Missing Missile", in which the star player of the Montreal Canadiens is kidnapped, which would be sort of like snatching the Pope out of Vatican City.

Television and ad writers abound. Radio station DJ's show up frequently. The hero of "Funny Man" yearns to be a stand-up comic. Professor Harry Lawson is a retired stage magician. And then, of course, there are the musicians.

Ellery Queen once wrote, "No one in the genre writes about music better than William Bankier." Several stories in this collection bear eloquent testimony to that. Bankier's life-long love affair with music is reflected in some of his finest work, including his 1980 Edgar Award nominated masterpiece "The Choirboy". In occasional pieces such as "Murder at the O'Shea Chorale", the tone is comedic. Most often, however, music forms the soundtrack of a tragedy. Each musical story becoming a song in the key of death.

The types of music involved, each described with passionate understanding and palpable affection, range from jazz to pop, classical to chorale. "Music has always been important to me... I sang in church choirs for many years...I love jazz and taught myself to play the clarinet and tenor saxophone, but I let them slip. Today, I play recorder by ear. My big number is "I Can't Get Started".

The diversity of Bankier's stories is as impressive as the output. Humour and suspense, whodunits and character studies, historical recreations and contemporary shock endings. The real mystery is why, with almost 200 stories to his credit, this is the first collection of Bankier's stories to be published. Welcome then, to the world of William Bankier. A world where nightmare comes silently, in the dead of night. Where the last act is often deadly. Where fear is a killer. Now turn the page and enter a bar where the patrons demonstrate Bankier's finely tuned ear for the lyrical, almost musical way people speak. Listen and find out what happens in Act One...

Toronto, Ontario, Canada
March, 1995

Postscript

On January 10, 1914, William Bankier died in Los Angeles. Behind him, in addition to a career spanning 50 years and hundreds of published stories, Bill also left behind loving family, devoted friends, admiring fans and story fragments, outlines and completed manuscripts intended for publication after his death. Bill was a consummate professional, a witty, charming man and a constantly inquiring mind. Although his output slackened in the last few years, every work he produced maintained the high Bankier standard. His love of music remained, along with his ability to find menace in the mundane and unexpected nightmare in any waking moment. Adios, Bill. You will be missed.

Toronto, Ontario, Canada
August, 2014

The Choirboy

Originally published in *Alfred Hitchcock Mystery Magazine*, June 1980.

THE MUSICIANS HAD TAPED THEIR TRACKS AND DEPARTED the studio, heading for wherever musicians go in Toronto on a July morning. Now Barry Latchford was alone in the soundproof room, adding his voice to the prerecorded background.

In the control room, Norman Inch pressed the intercom button. "You're a disappointment, Barry," he said.

Latchford was a sinewy man in his thirties with shoulder length blond hair and a sinister-looking mustache. Padded earphones gripped his head. He wore a striped freight-engineer's cap to go with his vagabond outfit of leather vest and stovepipe jeans. His boots were army surplus—parachute corps.

Barry Latchford resembled more a villain out of a spaghetti western than the best singer of TV and radio commercial music in Canada. The drummer on the gig had been awarded the laugh of the morning when he said Latchford looked like a tall angry Muppet.

When the producer from the advertising agency told him he was a disappointment, Latchford sat erect while a jolt of fear emptied his eyes. "What's the problem?" He was perfectionist enough to believe that criticism was always justified. Once, years ago, he had become a hermit for weeks, practicing his scales and breathing to be ready for the December night when the choir would perform the Messiah.

Behind the glass, Inch put a hand on the shoulder of his companion, Steve Pullman, the copywriter. "We were hoping we could stretch this session into an extra day," he said, his voice booming through the speaker. "But if you keep delivering the goods on the first take, we'll be on our way back to Montreal tonight."

Latchford relaxed. He slipped off the stool, eased the "cans" from his head, and hung them on the music stand.

"My wife complains about the same thing," he said. "I'm fabulous but I'm a little too quick."

"We'll hear a playback of everything so far," Inch proclaimed, "then we'll buy you a drink."

They went into a place near the studio. After drinking and talking baseball for a few minutes, Pullman said to Inch, "Tell Barry the idea. Let's not waste time."

"Mysterioso," Latchford said, taking an invisible sip of whisky.

"We write songs," Inch said dogmatically. "You've never heard of us because our commercial success to date has been the square root of nothing at all."

"Welcome to the club."

"Come on, you were in the charts with 'Apple Dreams' a couple of years ago."

"The Canadian charts—and even that was a struggle. I've never made it with a pop single in the U.S."

"So let's get together and create some prosperity," Pullman said. "Tell him the idea, Norman."

"The idea is you come down to Montreal and record one of our songs."

Latchford could feel remorse rising about him like ground mist in a horror film. God protect him from amateur songwriters. "Cutting a side is an expensive business," he said in the gloomy voice of a businessman.

Pullman's impatience was beginning to peak. "Will you tell him the idea, Norman?"

"We do it through my company, Inchworm Productions. The recording studio will be Carlo's—he owes us a couple of favors, so there'll be no studio charges. As for musicians, we do it on half scale. If the song takes off, everybody gets paid."

Latchford looked for a way out. "I'll have to check it out with Carol. My wife—she's my business manager."

·"Do it and let us know as soon as you can." Inch directed glances around the room like a marked man watching out for assassins.

"Even if you make the record and it's okay," Latchford persisted, "you're only half way there. If the stations won't play it, you're dead."

"Leave that to me," Pullman said. "I worked for three years as a DJ at CBAY."

"Baytown?" Years ago, on vacation, Latchford had spent an eventful thirty seconds driving through the town.

"The voice of Crystal Bay," Pullman intoned, cupping his ear pseudo-professionally. "I know how the hit parade can be rigged."

"Providing it's a good song," Latchford said. "You can't sell garbage."

"We won't give you garbage to record," Inch said patiently. "Be a good boy and check with your wife."

Carol Latchford sat at the kitchen table in one of the old cinema seats Barry had bought when the neighborhood Palace gave up and became a block of shops. Four maroon-plush recliners were now bolted to the vinyl floor, two on either side of the low pine table.

"I think you should record their song," Carol said. She was drinking beer from a bottle and smoking a thin brown cigarette.

Latchford was playing around with a wok on the gas stove, throwing in green peppers and mushrooms and slivers of chicken, being a virtuoso chef. "These are two little businessmen from the minor leagues," he said. "The writer is from Baytown—do you believe that? It's amateur night."

"What are you doing otherwise that's so important?" Carol was a short plump woman in her late twenties. She had a pussycat mouth, a turned-up nose, and green eyes with brows that arched in permanent astonishment. If faces had to be assigned countries, hers was Irish. "Something may come of it. You never can tell."

"You don't know these guys," Latchford insisted.

"Take me to meet them then," she said, finishing her beer, dropping the empty bottle into the case on the floor at her feet and flicking out a full one with a deft backhand movement.

Latchford frowned at the hiss of the bottlecap. "Could you manage to be sober if I did?"

"I can't remember the last time you took me somewhere."

"That's where you have the advantage. I can remember."

"Loosen up then. Have a drink with me—we'll have some fun."

"You call this fun?"

Steve Pullman was setting out a meager bar in Inch's hotel room: a bottle of Scotch, a bottle of gin, some tonic, four glasses, and a bucket of ice. "Why couldn't they ask us up to their place?" he whined. He felt poor, as if he was back in his parents' shabby house near the bay.

"His wife probably wanted to come out," Inch said. He was accustomed to pacifying his partner. Writers were all the same—if they weren't bitching about how terrible everything was, they were going over the top with enthusiasm over some minor success.

"I don't think he likes our idea," Pullman said.

"Then we'll sell it to him."

"Maybe we should line up another singer."

"Latchford's the best. We agreed we'd start with the best."

"I'm worried about how we finish," Pullman said grimly.

The Latchfords arrived in a mood of manufactured euphoria. Carol was wearing a crimson-silk jersey dress and charcoal nylons above plastic shoes without backs. Pullman fell in love with her legs immediately. He ordered the beer she requested and, when it came and he had opened one, placed himself where he could see every one of the frequent crossings of those smooth, shiny legs.

Everybody except Latchford drank a lot and the party was a reasonable success. By midnight when they were devouring room-service sandwiches and Carol was into her seventh pint of beer, Pullman was referring to her as the small-town girl. She was like the girls he remembered from the tea dances in the gymnasium at Baytown High School. Carol was flattered. "Let this guy write your lyrics, Barry," she said. "He's a magician with words."

Latchford tossed his head back, pretending to laugh without actually producing any sound.

In the taxi on the way home he grumbled, "I should go see a psychiatrist, agreeing to do this."

"We'll go to Montreal. We'll have some fun for a few days," Carol said. Her head was back on the upholstery, her eyes closed. "What can you lose?"

"You'll have fun. I saw you encouraging that bush-league lover. I should put you across my knee."

"Right now, I'd be grateful for even that."

Flora Inch, Norman's wife, selected the song that Latchford would record. She came out of her study in the bungalow across the river in St. Lambert with the portable cassette player in one hand and a page of notes in the other. "Here's my choice," she said.

" 'Summer Silence,' " Norman read from the list. He tried not to look too pleased. "I like that one too."

Flora moved a flower pot so she could perch on a window ledge. Her broad shape obscured most of the view of the Montreal highrise panorama in the distance. Richelieu, a tiny dog of indeterminate breed, limped from the kitchen, saw the woman he loved, took a skittering run, and leaped onto a lap that barely existed. Flora saved the dog from falling and cuddled it to her tank-topped bosom. She had the shoulders of a Channel swimmer, the cropped hair of a woman who wants a rest. Her face was as pretty as a doll's.

"Richie, Richie," she crooned. Then, after a pause in which her eyes went out of focus, "The lyric could use a little fixing. Would you like me to do it?"

"I don't want a hassle with Steve."

"You want a good lyric. Steve Pullman has blind spots. I know—I wrote copy in the next office for three years."

"You may be right, but leave it alone. We have a delicate operation here. Stay home and write your novel."

"God help me, I've written it three times. Let me up."

"You're the one who cried out for artistic freedom. Write the book."

"I'm coming to that recording session. I'm not going to miss the rematch between Latchford's wife and our little Stevie!"

Carlo's Recording Center was a compact set of rooms engineered and hand-built by the owner. Carlo sat at the console, straight-backed, Spanish eyes alert, watching Barry Latchford through the glass partition as if the singer might fly at any minute and it would be his responsibility to trap him in a net. Norman Inch lounged beside Carlo in the producer's chair.

Steve Pullman and the two women were crowded onto the visitors' settee. Flora Inch had always been like a sister to Steve, taking him under her wing on his first day at the ad agency. She sat on his left now, bending occasionally to feed a chocolate tidbit to the carpet remnant she called a dog. "This is your best work, Steve," she commented after the first take. "Be proud of this song."

On his right, Carol Latchford crossed her legs, bringing a stiletto heel down across Pullman's trousers. "Sorry," she said, brushing her hand firmly and repeatedly over his calf.

By the third take, everybody agreed Latchford had done his best. Carlo had a paying client coming in, so the session had to end. "Everybody come over to St. Lambert," Flora said briskly, scooping up Richelieu. "Can we all squeeze into my car?"

They straggled out of the control room. "Looks like you're on my lap, Carol," Pullman said.

Inch directed a weak grin at Barry Latchford, who looked right through him as he unwrapped two sticks of gum and stuffed them into his mouth.

Flora Inch's food was late but meanwhile the wine flowed and the house filled with the aroma of roasting beef and salad dressing spiked with garlic and dry mustard. When the inebriated guests sat down at the table and fell on the meal, they all told the hostess it was the most delicious they had ever eaten.

"Have some more beef, Steve," Flora said. She was drifting to and from the kitchen beyond a waist-high divider lined with a cherry cheesecake and a pecan pie. "I don't want to end up feeding sirloin to that piggy Richelieu."

"You aren't eating, Barry," Inch scolded the singer.

"I'm always down after a session," Latchford mumbled, looking into space. "Don't mind me."

"Don't mind him," Carol echoed. "Barry-baby will retire to the wilderness shortly and communicate with his inner spirit. One Magnificat, two Te Deums, and a fast chorus of Panis Angelicus, and he'll be as good as new."

"Don't give that lady any more to drink," Latchford said with a false smile.

"Are you a choirboy?" Flora asked. "I used to pipe away with the altos at St. James the Apostle on Ste. Catherine Street. If this was Saturday night, we could drive over tomorrow morning for matins."

"I wouldn't mind that," Latchford said, his pale eyes staring through the window into the twinkling black mass of the Montreal skyline.

In the weeks that followed, after the Barry Latchford recording of "Summer Silence" was released, some of the euphoria began to wear off. They had a good song, but pessimism arose as they listened to it for the 150th time. Inch lifted the tone arm. "Where do we go from here?" he said. They were using the agency studio for their private business.

"To church," Pullman said drily, "like your wife keeps saying. Only we go to pray, not to sing."

"Pray, hell. The whole idea, your idea, is that we don't leave things to chance."

"It's in the lap of the gods."

"You were going to rig the charts. Line up a crowd of little girls to phone the stations all day asking for Barry Latchford's new single."

"It isn't that easy. Latchford's nobody to these kids. They only request what everybody else is requesting—Michael Jackson, the Bee Gees."

"Pay them then."

"It gets complicated. What if some parents wonder where the kids are getting the money? Our involvement comes out, Latchford looks terrible, and so do Inch and Pullman."

"Why didn't you think of this in the beginning?"

"I was being optimistic. Forgive me."

The telephone rang beside Inch. He picked it up. "Studio."

"A call from Toronto, Mr. Inch. Barry Latchford."

"Put him on." He said to Pullman, "It's Russ Columbo. Our troubles are just beginning."

Pullman closed his eyes and sighed.

"We were just talking about you, Barry. Did you get the record I sent you?" Inch listened for half a minute. "Feel free to do whatever you can to promote it up there. Meanwhile, we're going ahead as discussed." When the call was finished, Inch let the telephone drop into its cradle as if it was something wet.

"He's over the moon," he said. "We'd better produce some evidence that we're trying to sell his song."

In Toronto, Barry Latchford went through the house looking for Carol. He found her in the television room. The set was playing with the sound off. She was placed in a chair in viewing position, trying to read a newspaper by the light from the screen. Her knitting rested on the carpet. Beside it was an ashtray full of cigarette ends and an empty beer bottle.

"Your trouble is you don't have anything to do," he said.

"Wrong," she said. "It says here Imperial Tobacco and Molson's Brewery have increased production. I'll never catch up."

He sat on the floor. "That sounds like an unhappy woman."

"You always had a good ear."

He took the newspaper from her and snapped off the television, leaving only one source of light—the lamp in the hall outside the open door. "I really don't like to see you unhappy."

"I'm sorry. I can't please you with satisfaction I don't possess." She lit another cigarette. "It probably isn't your fault. Different things make us happy. I like dance halls—they call them discos now—and I hardly ever see the inside of one. I'd like to wear some of those wild leather clothes the kids are into, but you'd think I was crazy."

He looked away, hoping she wouldn't go on. If she turned herself into one of those freaks he couldn't imagine how he'd react.

"You fooled me. First time I saw you singing in the club I thought you were a swinger. We should never have got married." She blew a fierce shaft of smoke.

"Are you in love with that writer character?"

Carol picked up her knitting, held the needles poised, and stared at the particle of space between their tips. "Steve Pullman? Am I in love with him? Not quite."

"He never takes his eyes off you."

"Better not say that. You're making me all excited."

"He wants to take you away to Baytown or wherever the hell he comes from."

"Small-town bliss. Now there's a dream."

Latchford put a firm hand on his wife's knee. "Don't leave me, Carol."

"Message noted," she said, and the knitting needles began to click like a machine.

The Montreal promotion never did get off the ground. But as things turned out Pullman's failure to deliver didn't matter. Latchford took his copy of "Summer Silence" to a DJ friend at the top station in Toronto. He loved it, played it three times on one morning show, and the telephone began to ring. The process didn't stop for two months as the song reached the top of the charts and stayed there. The distributor told the factory to press another 50,000, and began spreading the word to radio stations and dealers across Canada. He also telephoned a connection in New York. They had a phenomenon on their hands—a song that couldn't fail to make it big.

Indian summer is always a special time in Montreal. Bonfires send pungent smoke trailing upward into hazy blue skies. The bittersweet afternoons are silent in memory of the days of warmth and comfort that are gone forever.

Barry and Carol Latchford came down for the celebration at the Inch residence on the south shore. It was clearly time to open the champagne; the record was now the top-selling single in the history of Canadian pop music. Better still, a deal was set for distribution in the States. Latchford's dream had come true.

The party was one of those Saturday affairs where the few people not invited turn up anyway, bringing bottles as admission. Every room was crowded, as were the back garden, the front lawn, the stairs, the garage, even the cars parked in the driveway. All the doors were open, the music system was on full volume; the sophisticated party dominated the entire neighborhood.

Norman Inch finally managed to manoeuvre his wife out of the kitchen and into a quiet corner. "I'm worried about Steve," he said.

"I told him not to follow wine with beer."

"I mean the way he keeps after Carol Latchford. Barry's starting to look at him."

Flora's eyes grew large and innocent. "So?"

"So all we need is a fistfight between the guest of honor and the lyricist."

"It might be just what the party needs."

"I don't know why I bother talking to you."

"People should be allowed to go where their actions take them. It helps the plot develop."

"These are not characters in your bloody novel."

"Real people can live or die just like fictional characters." Flora blinked at her husband. "And I don't like your tone of voice. My novel one day will surpass any of your so-called successes with chintzy songs about summer love."

By two o'clock on Sunday morning the police had paid two polite visits, the music was now turned low, most of the guests had gone home, and those few who remained were caged inside the house. The Latchfords had come with luggage for a long week-end. Barry had removed his turtleneck sweater and suede jacket some time after midnight and was now wearing his pajama top. He was sitting on a couch beside his hostess, swallowing cognac from a tumbler.

"We've got to do it, Barry," Flora said. She crossed her legs and Richelieu repositioned himself on her lap without opening his eyes.

"Do what?" Latchford was looking through a doorway at his wife dancing with Pullman in the next room. Carol was a lot shorter than

Steve; her cheek was pressed against his chest, her skirt riding up in back, showing plenty of rounded calf. Pullman's chin rested on the top of her curly head. He saw Latchford watching them and gave him a sleepy grin.

"We have to go to St. James the Apostle tomorrow morning," Flora said. "We have to show them how to sing."

"I haven't been to church in ten years," he said.

Latchford and his brothers had been the foundation of the choir for a long time. When they matured and went professional, their gospel quartet was good enough to hold a radio series on the Dominion Network. They even did a summer series on television. His chance to go single, to do club dates, had seemed like the beginning of a fabulous career. Now, even with the U.S. hit in the pipeline, he found himself longing for the uncomplicated delight of standing around the piano with his brothers rehearsing "This Little Light of Mine."

"You haven't been to church in ten years? I haven't been in twenty. I'd say we're both overdue." Flora followed Barry's gaze to see what was distracting him. She raised her glass and her voice. "Yoo-hoo, Stevie! Here's to young love!"

Later, Inch was unloading a tray of glasses in the kitchen. The party had gone quiet. Suddenly Latchford's voice rang out in a tone heavy with warning. "Steve!"

The command was so threatening Inch's heart began to pound. He moved quickly from the kitchen into the room that had been cleared for dancing. Nobody was there. Through the door way he could see a tableau at the couch in the front room. Latchford had risen, his glass in one hand, his eyes focused on the French doors leading to the garden. Flora was holding a restraining hand on his wrist while she pressed Richelieu down on her lap. The dog's ears were up—he was tense, alert.

After this frozen moment, things began to move quickly. Latchford broke away, dropping the glass on the carpet and vanishing swiftly through the French doors. Flora struggled up and the dog went scampering.

"What's happening?"

"Steve and Carol stopped dancing and went out back."

Inch showed his wife a hopeless face. "I'm not happy stopping fights."

"Steve has it coming. He's been socking it in with that little slut all evening."

Carol Latchford's voice rang out in the garden. "Don't you start, Barry—I'm warning you!" Then she screamed "Stop! Somebody stop him!"

When Inch reached the end of the garden he could hardly see in the darkness. He could faintly make out Latchford's pajama clad arm rising and falling as he knelt across Steve Pullman. Forcing himself to intervene, he put a hand on Barry's shoulder. It was like touching a button on a machine. The beating ended abruptly and Latchford sat back on his haunches.

"Call the police," Carol said. Her voice was outraged, like that of a parent who has seen a child go too far.

Inch's eyes were accustomed to the darkness now. He leaned down and looked at what had been Steve Pullman's face. "We need an ambulance," he said.

Latchford got up and walked away. He discovered he was holding a rock in his hand. He let it fall. Behind him he could hear the panic, the excitement, people running into each other, voices shouting, somebody trying to start a car and calling a girl to come on because he wanted to get going.

His arms ached. He remembered the day when he was ten years old and he tried to walk home from the supermarket carrying two paper bags of groceries against this chest. The bags seemed light enough at the start but before he was halfway home he knew he couldn't support them longer than another few seconds. There was no place to set them down and he felt such a sense of failure and embarrassment he began to cry. When he finally made it to the house, after spilling the contents of one of the bags in the gutter, his arms throbbed for the rest of the afternoon.

The lights of Inch's house were getting farther away. Latchford turned and blundered back through a low hedge, across a flower bed. He went inside and hurried up the stairs to the guest room, where he stripped off the blood-spattered pajama top and changed into a shirt. He paused, then felt impelled to put on a necktie and his suede jacket.

As he was leaving the house by the front door, he was confronted by Carol. Her face was streaked with tears and dirt. "Where are you going? The police are coming."

"Bye-bye, Carol."

"You're crazy."

"I told you to stop fooling around."

"Why did you keep hitting him? Once was enough."

"Why did you drink so much?"

She held him by the arm as he tried to walk away. He twisted free, feeling skin from his forearm collecting under her fingernails as he released himself. "Feel better?"

"Where are you going?'

Latchford had no idea.

He followed curving streets and found himself close to the river. The metropolis lay on the other side, humming, vibrating like a starship just landed after a voyage across the universe. To his right, a gigantic bridge connected the south shore with the city. He began walking in that direction.

Halfway across the bridge, he stopped and stared out at the night past a barrier of steel struts and girders. He was like a prisoner in a cage, but he felt safe, protected rather than confined. The considerable amount of alcohol he had consumed was beginning to wear off. Latchford realized now, for the first time, that he had deliberately killed Steve Pullman, beaten him to death, murdered him. He tried to recall the event but it wasn't clear in his mind. He had a suspicion he had enjoyed it.

Carol's question had been "Why did you keep hitting him?" Latchford stood in his cage and tried to think of an answer. Hardly a day went by in which he was not tense as a spring, racing from here to there, doing what everybody else wanted, singing their nonsensical jingles, taking their money and their praise when he knew he was guilty of conspiring to produce rubbish.

What should he be doing then? What sort of life would have converted him into a satisfied man who did not beat rivals to death at parties? The days of singing with his brothers—were those not happy times? Latchford tried to recapture the feeling that went with standing around the piano in the family living room, harmonizing gospel hymns —"Throw Out The Lifeline," "What a Friend We Have in Jesus." The memory of the music brought tears to his eyes but he could identify no sense of inner peace from that faraway life.

Perhaps he had always been driven to go further and try new things. Maybe that was why he'd left the quartet and pursued a commercial career. Latchford didn't really understand why he did what he did. For as long as he could remember, he had been carrying a giant rage. Maybe he deserved credit for containing it till now. The question was not really why he had killed but how everybody else kept the blood off their hands.

A giant bus frightened him as it hissed its brakes going past on the road behind him. With his heart pounding, Latchford began walking toward the city.

The police arrived at the Inch residence promptly and were disturbed to learn that the assailant had been allowed to walk away from the scene. They took a description and spent half an hour checking out the neighborhood gardens with flashlights.

"He's miles away by now," one of them said with satisfaction as they slammed the doors of the police car and followed the ambulance carrying Pullman's body.

Nobody slept. By nine-thirty in the morning Flora had washed three loads of dishes. Carol was drying and stacking. Norman was sitting at the table, smoking, staring out the window at the glorious morning, shaking his head solemnly every now and then, like a baseball pitcher shrugging off his catcher's signals. They were all waiting for the phone to ring.

At last Carol said, "Can we have the radio on?"

Norman reached out and snapped the switch of the transistor. An announcer read the weather, gave the time, then an organ played an introduction and a lugubrious male voice began to sing.

> "Sweet hour of prayer, sweet hour of prayer
> That calls us from a world of care..."

Flora raised her head from the detergent bubbles. "I know where Barry is," she said. "He's at church."

"He hasn't gone since we've been married," Carol said.

"I told him last night about St. James the Apostle." She began drying her hands.

"I'll get the car out," Norman said.

"No, I'll drive myself. You haven't shaved."

"Wouldn't it be better to call the police?" Carol said.

Flora stared at her, then turned to the door. "Wash your face, child. We're going to find your husband and bring him home."

In the car, Carol said, "I guess I sounded inhuman back there."

"My husband has never killed anybody," Flora said, "so I don't know how I'd behave in your place." She gunned illegally past a line of cars on the bridge. "As far as I know he's never killed anybody."

"It can't get any worse for me. I've been misrable for most of the last six years. Barry is bound to go to jail for a long time and I know I'll be happier without him." They were off the bridge now, moving through the narrow streets of east Montreal. "I'm a bitch, eh?"

Flora gave Carol a speculative glance. "Yes, I'd say a bitch."

Parking spaces were plentiful on a Sunday morning. Flora stopped on Crescent Street, locked the car, then led the way at a fast pace toward the gray-stone church. The fine weather showed no signs of breaking. Flora's cream straw hat sparkled in the sunlight. She had offered to lend a hat to Carol but the Torontonian declined and wrapped her head in a scarf. Small-town girl, was Flora's assessment of that decision.

They were just in time for the service. The church was filled. An usher helped them cram into a pew near the back. Flora, a choir-trained Anglican, genuflected and said a silent prayer, then sat back. In every direction she saw massed heads and shoulders. Carol leaned close to whisper, "We'll never find him, even if he is here."

"Don't worry, he's here."

The service began with the choir chanting what to Flora were familiar notes, but there was no response from the congregation so she remained silent. Then the minister announced the opening hymn and as the organ played the seventeenth-century tune, "Nun Danket," the congregation and choir rose, shuffling and coughing.

> "Now thank we all our God,
> With heart and hands and voices...."

It was at the beginning of the second verse that she realized something unusual was happening. The congregation had fallen silent and many of the choir members had their eyes raised to the balcony. Above her, out of Flora's sight, Barry Latchford was singing as if it had been rehearsed this way.

> "Oh, may this bounteous God
> Through all our life be near us..."

Gradually the choir stopped singing until, by the last quatrain, it was Barry alone accompanied by the organ. His tone was fuller than anything Flora had heard in Carlo's studio all those months ago. She felt she was listening to a different voice.

> "And keep us in His grace,
> And guide us when perplexed,
> And free us from all ills
> In this world and the next."

The women waited for Latchford in the sunlight outside the church. He made no attempt to walk away. He was unshaven and red-eyed but he was smiling. This boyish smile was different from the cynical one Flora had come to think of as typically Latchford. Carol didn't move to him nor did he approach her.

Flora watched them for a few seconds, squinting into the sun. "Let's go home," she said at last.

"Are the police there?"

"No. I thought we'd have lunch, you can clean up and rest for a while, then we'll call them."

He nodded. In the car he said, "Not a bad ending."

"What ending?" Flora said. "You won't be in forever. You'll come out and start singing the proper music, the way you sang this morning."

"I don't think so."

"Why not?"

"I killed that man. All he did was play a little game with Carol and I took his life. That can't be right."

The police took Latchford away at four. By five, Carol had departed in a taxi for the airport, refusing a lift. The house was tidy—Norman had been busy. He came into Flora's study carrying two drinks; she was in her swivel chair, staring at the typewriter.

Norman handed her a glass and sat down. "I wouldn't want to go through that again," he said.

"You won't. Not with Steve, anyway."

"I could do without the smart answers. He was my partner."

"You'll find somebody better. Carol will settle down with a small-town boy who suits her. Latchford will sing the roof off the prison chapel. Everybody's ahead."

"Except Steven Pullman."

The telephone rang and Norman went down the hall to answer it. When he came back a couple of minutes later, the glass in his hand was empty. "That was somebody from the police. Latchford is dead."

"I don't believe it." Flora looked stunned. "What happened?"

"They didn't handcuff him because he was so quiet, the way he gave himself up. In the station he knocked over a cop, managed to get hold of his gun, and turned it on himself."

Flora reached under the desk and lifted Richelieu from the basket. She cradled him on her lap, rocking back and forth in the swivel chair.

"That's how right you were about Latchford," Norman said bitterly. "I wonder about the rest of us."

Making a Killing with Mama Cass

Originally published in *Alfred Hitchcock Mystery Magazine*, January 1980.

"WHY WEREN'T YOU AT THE AIRPORT?" GARY PRIME SAID to his wife Anitra as she let herself into the apartment. "The car would have made sense. Instead I was stuck with an eight-dollar taxi." This was about as much anger as Gary ever expressed.

"I got your wire but Lee had important clients in the screening room. I had to be there." Anitra glanced at herself in a mirror, wondering if her adventure had made any visible difference. Gary back a day early was all she needed. She could have used more time to compose herself, to decide where they were all going from here—herself and Gary and Lee Cosford.

"Busy while I was away?" Gary asked.

"As usual. How was London?"

"I enjoyed it." This was not the whole truth. Gary was a good mixer—his job demanded it. As a salesman for a Montreal engraving house, calling on the production departments of ad agencies, he got on well with the men who could discuss the advantages of offset reproduction versus letterpress. But throw him in with the clever boys from the creative department and it wasn't the same.

He was grateful for his free trip to England even though he knew he'd been asked only because somebody dropped out at the last minute. His engravings were the backbone of the prize-winning campaign, therefore some Samaritan had suggested filling the vacant seat with good old Gary. He had asked Anitra to come along but she refused, pleading too much going on at Lee Cosford Productions.

"I enjoyed London," Gary repeated, "except for some of the brilliant conversation. My idea of hell is to be locked up for twenty-four hours with two copywriters, an art director, and an unlimited supply of booze. --The drunker they get, the more they laugh. Only I can't see the joke half the time." Gary suspected that sometimes they derived their amusement from him. Not that he was a clod: his suit cost two hundred dollars, his shoes were shined, and he kept his hair trimmed. Maybe it was the haircut. The creative types either let their heads go altogether or had it styled and sprayed so they looked like Glen Campbell.

"Pay no attention to them," Anitra said. She was pouring herself some coffee from the pot Gary had made when he came in. She looked good against the counter in slim denims made stylish by a gold belt. "Agency guys are all the same. They think they're some kind of elite."

"Elite. That's the word. Everything is a put-down. You don't dare tell them you enjoyed a movie--they'll say it was commercial and leave you feeling stupid. To hear them, the girls going by are all dogs or hustlers, the food in the restaurant contains the 'permissable level' of rodent hairs, and the wine is sulphuric acid."

"Kill-joys."

"That's the word for them. Kill-joys. If you have a sincere feeling you have to hide it or they'll make it into a joke."

"So you had a lousy time. At least it was free." Anitra studied her husband. Something was on his mind. He could never conceal enthusiasm—it shone from the large square face, the jaw set firm, the thick black hair neatly combed and gleaming with Vitalis.

"It was only two days and apart from the meals I was usually on my own." He was getting ready to tell her. "But there was a thing happened --I'm excited about it. It's as if..."

When Gary finished talking, Anitra could not understand what he was so worked up about. He had been watching late-night television in his hotel room and had turned on a talk show. The guest was the English actress Donna Dean, the sex symbol from the sixties, who was still pretty today but hugely overweight.

Anitra said, "And your idea is what? You want to ask her to be in a film about Mama Cass?"

"Not me. I can't ask her. A film producer has to ask her. But she'd be perfect—if you saw her you'd know what I mean. She's blonde, of course, so she'd need a dark wig. But she has the same baby face as Mama Cass and that majestic build. She was even wearing one of those big tent dresses Cass used to wear --"

Anitra found it difficult to become interested. Years ago, she had enjoyed listening to The Mamas and The Papas and she had agreed with Gary in those days that the bell-like voice of Cass Elliott had a lot to do with the group's success. More recently, she had heard something about the young woman's untimely death, but nothing much about it had registered. "O.K., there could be a film in it," Anitra said. "What's it got to do with you?"

"I'm the one to make it happen. I've got to do it."

After watching the Donna Dean interview, Gary had left the hotel and gone for a walk along Bayswater Avenue. It was midnight. Hyde Park was on his right, substantial white Edwardian buildings on his left. Ahead loomed Marble Arch and Park Lane with its lineup of hotels far posher than the one he was inhabiting. Noisy little cars, square black taxis, and an occasional red double-decker bus kept up a continuous roar beside him, but Gary hardly heard the traffic.

His mind was filled with music from the cassettes he used to play till they nearly fell apart, the songs of dreams and of young girls coming to the canyon.

According to the newspapers, Cass Elliott had died in a hotel somewhere near there. They said she choked to death on a sandwich alone in her room.

"I have to get the film going," Gary told his wife. "And now. Something tells me it's important."

"If you say so."

"Your boss said once that a feature film will never happen unless somebody puts all his energy behind it. There are too many other ideas competing for the funds and the facilities."

"Lee should know."

"Right. So I thought you might lay it on him tomorrow."

"Me? It's your idea." The last two days at Lee's place had given Anitra a shaking up. Some change in the relationship had been coming for a long time. But now she felt uncertain about her future and the sensation was distasteful to her. From the time eight years ago when she organized her marriage to Gary, Anitra had kept uncertainties to a minimum. The false pregnancy was a cheat but it got her out of a dismal situation at home. And it had done Gary no harm; he was forever testifying that the unexpected marriage had stabilized his life.

Now, for the sake of some excitement, she had gone with Lee Cosford. The event was satisfying enough as it was happening, but when they parted there had been a distant look in Lee's pale eyes and Anitra was no fool.

"You'd better describe the idea to Lee yourself," she said. "I wouldn't do it justice." It would kill her to approach him with this loony request, as if she thought he owed her something.

"Just mention it. Set it up for me."

"You're a big boy, Gary. You know his number. Call him and tell him you've got a business proposition. Lee Cosford would rather talk business than anything."

Lee Cosford, rotund and dynamic, rolled out into the waiting room and took Gary by the arm. "Stranger," he said laughing, eyeing Prime anxiously, "where've you been keeping yourself? Come in and sit down. Stephie, make us a couple of coffees, will you?"

The idea sounded even better to Gary as he described it in Lee Cosford's panelled office, taking pulls at a huge mug of coffee, squinting against sunlight streaming through the window past the spire of a church on lower Mountain Street. Cosford lay back in his leather recliner, boots on the glass desk, eyes closed like a man in a barber chair. As Gary finished, the bells in the tower across the street began to peal. He thought it was a good omen.

Cosford opened one eye. "Is that it?"

"That's it Lee."

The film producer sat up. "I think it's a sensational idea."

"Really?"

"Fabulous. And you've probably heard Anitra mention I want to get into feature films. You can't know how soul-destroying it is producing thirty-second pieces of film to sell detergent or sausages. Or maybe you do know. You have the same assignment in print."

"I know what you mean." Actually, Gary was proud of the engravings his firm produced.

"The trouble is," Cosford said, "there are too many good film ideas chasing too little money. You just can't get the financing."

"I thought there was this Canadian Film Development Council. Don't they put up money?"

"That's right." Cosford put his knees under the desk and folded his arms precisely on the cold glass. This square individual in the overpressed suit had managed to brief himself. "The CFDC will, on occasion, back a good idea."

"And this is more than a good idea, Lee. It's a great idea."

"Right." Cosford's mind was working fast. He was more than ready to see the last of Gary Prime. "But there's only one way to approach the Council. They have to see a treatment."

"Treatment?"

"Right." Cosford picked up his telephone, consulted a page of names and numbers, and began to dial. "A scenario - an outline of what the film is going to be about."

"Can't we just put the idea down in a letter?"

"No, it has to be professionally done. And I've got just the man to do it." Cosford straightened up and smiled into the phone. "Hello, Lucas? Did I wake you? Lee Cosford. Fine, how are you? Luke, facing me across my desk is a bright-eyed, bushy-tailed fellow named Gary Prime who happens to have a sensational idea for a feature film. The idea is so good, the only person to do the treatment is Lucas Pennington."

After Gary Prime went away with an appointment to see Pennington at his apartment that afternoon, Lee Cosford wandered through a maze of corridors till he came to a small room where his film editor was seated at a Steenbeck machine with Anitra Prime at his shoulder. They were peering into the frosted glass screen at the image of a child holding a doll. The editor spun the film backward, then forward again so that the child kissed the doll while Anitra clicked her stopwatch.

"I just had your husband in. Thanks for not warning me."

"I would have guessed next week. He's quick off the mark all of a sudden."

"Never mind. I got rid of him."

"He's sincere about the idea."

"I have twenty-five sincere ideas for feature films. Nine of them are my own." Cosford opened a window and spat out into a laneway three floors below. He watched the spittle float down to disappear onto grey pavement. "I sent him to Lucas Pennington to get a treatment done."

The bald-headed man at the editing machine laughed.

"Who's Lucas Pennington?" Anitra asked.

"Before your era. Once a good copywriter, now a professional drunk. He's a freelance with loads of free time. Which is another way of saying the agencies are tired of Pennington missing deadlines."

Anitra said, "It sounds like a dirty trick, Lee." She frowned at her stopwatch; she was having no end of trouble making the product shot time out properly.

"It's dirty but effective. It gets Gary off my back while he and poor old Luke use up a year pretending they're writing a movie."

It was half past two when Gary showed up at Lucas Pennington's place on Bleury Street. The apartment was located up a flight of uncarpeted stairs above a tavern and a shop that sold sneezing powder and rubber excrement. When he heard the knock, Pennington put the gin bottle and his glass out of sight--not because he was an inhospitable man, but because there was barely enough for himself. He left magazines, newspapers, open books, soiled clothing, empty food tins and soft-drink bottles where they were and went to the door.

With his guest inside and seated, Pennington performed a humanitarian act; he opened a window.

Gary looked at the man who was supposed to write his Mama Cass treatment. To recommend this one, Lee Cosford had to be crazy. Pennington managed to be gaunt and sloppy at the same time. He seemed somewhere in his fifties—large head, patchy grey hair on a scalp that was scabby in places, apologetic eyes, and a smile that was choreographed to cover bad teeth. He had shaved a couple of days ago and had cut himself doing it.

"O.K. All right now. Right." He was rummaging around the room, not looking at Gary, sounding like a nervous infielder at the start of his final season. "Tell me about this picture of yours."

As Gary described his visit to London, his television glimpse of Donna Dean, and the flash of inspiration that led him to cast her in the role of his favorite singer, Pennington, who had discovered a notebook and a pen, lay on the floor with his head and shoulders against the baseboard, his eyes closed.

"So if Dean would agree to do it, and if we could get the right to use the original recordings for her to mime, the way the singers all do on TV these days," Gary concluded, "I think we could have a good film."

Pennington rolled sideways onto his elbow cupping his cheek in one hand. He bit the cover off the felt tipped pen he was holding, spat it away, and began flipping the pages of the notebook to find a clean one. They were all filled with indecipherable scrawl. At last he settled for half of the inside back cover. "Brilliant. Solid gold," he said as he tried to make marks with the pen. "Put me in, coach. Let me work on this one."

"You mean it?"

The writer turned his eyes up to Gary and they looked different—they looked angry and hungry, the apologetic wetness all gone. Pennington was feeling an old, almost -forgotten sensation, the one he used to experience in his first agency job when the new assignments came in and he couldn't wait to dazzle the copy chief and the account supervisor and the client with another brilliant idea. Quite often he would deliver a winner. Then it was cover the table with beer and how about a little more money for young Luke before Y&R lures him away with shares.

"I mean it all right," Pennington said. "You're onto a sure thing, my son. Mama Cass—that voice, the way she used to raise her hand and give that little half-salute as the song began to swing...I want to weep." The pen refused to write and, after tearing holes in the cover, he threw pen and notebook against the wall, struggling to his feet like a crippled, pregnant camel.

"The tragedy of her death." Pennington was pulling magazines and files from a buried tabletop, uncovering a typewriter. He used an ankle to drag a wooden chair into place, sat down, and cranked a crumpled letter around the roller, using two fingers to begin typing on the back of the paper. "What a career she had. Cass Elliott—there has to be a movie about her. And I know what you mean about the English broad to play the role. She's almost Cass's double. And she'll do a hell of a good job—never mind the silly parts they gave her in the sixties. She's a pro, a trained actress."

Pennington's typing was erratic. The keys kept sticking together in bunches and he cursed as he clawed them away from the paper. He squinted at what he had done. "This ribbon is dead. It's a ghost. Can you read that?"

Gary leaned over his shoulder, holding his breath. "Just barely."

"Never mind, it's coming, old son, the words are coming and I'll hammer the bastards down. Cosford knows my situation. He'll make a dark photostat of this and enlarge it three times." Pennington managed to hit several keys without an overlap and he laughed out loud. "The old rhythm," he said. "Once you've got it, you never lose it."

"Can I do anything to help?' Gary asked, delighted with this crazy old writer's reaction to his idea.

"Yes. Get out of here and let me work."

Two days later, Lucas Pennington showed up in the reception room of Lee Cosford Productions. The girl behind the board blinked at the sight of the very tall man in his dusty suit. It was a three-piece blue serge—not this year's model, not this decade's. At the top of it, above the frayed grey collar and badly knotted tie, was a wet, crimson face looking as if the man had just shaved it with a broken bottle. At the bottom, stepping forward awkwardly across the deep-pile carpet, were astonishing leather thong sandals over patterned socks.

Lee Cosford came out to claim his visitor. In the office he offered gin and Pennington accepted, saying, "First since day before yesterday. How about that, temperance fans?"

Cosford knew this had to be about the Gary Prime project. He believed he had heard the end of it but now here was the top writer from a generation ago looking as if he had just seen a vision on the road to Ste. Anne de Beaupré. Cosford reached out and took the glass away from his guest and said, "Tell me, Luke. Before you dive back into the sauce. Is there a feature film in this Mama Cass thing?"

"Academy Awards. Cannes Festival. The idea is solid gold, my dear. I've been working for two days on the treatment without anything to drink but coffee and grapefruit juice. It's in this brown envelope, Lee old buddy, and what you had better do is line up tons of money and hire your cast and your director because somewhere there's a lucky man who is going to make the film of the year from this here scenario of mine."

Cosford handed back the drink. "I just wanted to hear you say it." He took the envelope and went to sit behind his desk. To himself he said, always trust a sober Pennington. He drew a thick sheaf of typewritten pages from the envelope. "Wow, what did you do, write a shooting script?"

"Almost. I had to force myself not to. I even went out and invested in a ribbon and a box of paper." Pennington drew on the drink, then set it aside and looked out of the window at the church spire.

Cosford studied the title page. It said, "Blues for Mama Cass—a film drama with interpolated music. A Lee Cosford Production written by Lucas Pennington." The script had weight in Cosford's hands; it felt crisp and substantial—he knew the heft of valuable work. He flicked the title page over and saw the beginning of the treatment. The writing flowed. It was vintage Pennington.

The producer glanced up, wondering whether he should mention the fact that Gary Prime's name did not appear on the script. He decided to let it go for the moment.

"Do you want up-front money, Luke," he asked, "or would you rather take a share of the gross?"

Pennington made growling noises in his throat as he rubbed his hands together. "Some of each, please," he said and, out in the reception area, Stephie heard through the wall the deep, nasty sounds of her boss and his visitor laughing.

* * * *

Gary told Anitra how his project was going. He enthused over the meeting with Lucas Pennington, describing what a wash-out the man seemed to be, then how he came alight when the idea was explained. Aware of Pennington's bad reputation, knowing it was all a ploy to fob Gary off with a loser, Anitra was tempted to warn her husband not to expect too much. But why come on as a pessimist? Let the man have his dream for a while longer. Besides, you never could tell—something might come of it.

It was only by accident that she discovered a few weeks later that something was indeed coming of the Mama Cass project. Anitra encountered Stephie at the photocopy machine and happened to see that she was running off several copies of what looked like a shooting script. A glance at the title page and Anitra was off to see Lee Cosford almost at a run.

Then she slowed down, thinking, and stopped. The film business ground on at a steady pace at the best of times. No mad rush. She would wait and see what was going to happen next.

What happened was that Lee announced he was flying to London on business at the beginning of the week. He asked Stephie to book a couple of seats on the Air Canada flight for Sunday evening. If the other seat was for Gary, Anitra told herself, her husband would have been crowing before now. If it was for her, Lee would have said something. Instead, he was keeping his head down these days, acting as if he had done a lousy job of picking her pocket and hoped she wouldn't mention it.

Anitra decided to bring up the subject as she sat in the front seat of Lee's car driving back from the Eastern Townships where they had been filming a butter commercial. She was never so grateful for a safety belt as when she drove with Lee Cosford. The highway was fairly clear and he kept pushing the accelerator. The needle edged past eighty-five, ninety.

Suddenly the steering wheel began to shudder in Lee's hands. He straightened his arms, reducing speed. "Second time it's done that." He swore a couple of times but his eyes were bright. He was enjoying himself. "Something is wrong with this car, my dear. Anything over ninety and she tries to run away from me."

Anitra stopped bracing her feet against the floor and tried to relax, her heart still racing. "Lee," she said, "what the hell are you up to?"

"I like to drive fast," he said.

"I mean with Gary's idea. I saw the treatment Pennington wrote. You're getting ready to run with it."

"Luke says it has potential. He may be a lush but Pennington has judgment."

"But why isn't Gary's name on the front page? Why doesn't he even know you're going ahead?"

"He will, he will—don't worry about it. As soon as I get my financing organized I'll write Gary a nice check."

"Thanks very much. Good thing I brought it up."

Cosford glanced at her and back at the road. The speedometer crept upwards and a feathery vibration in the steering wheel tickled his fingers. "Anitra, you know the film business. Let's face it, your husband is just an engraver's rep. What does he know from films? This is a Lee Cosford Production. It has to be if it's going to work." He glanced over again and this time he encountered her eyes staring straight at him. It was a frightening sight. "Come on! Gary fluked an idea that happens to have possibilities. O.K., we're going to pay him for it. But the business of making it into a film is for me and Luke Pennington. And for you—you can be part of this too."

They drove a mile or two in silence.

Then he said breezily, "Want to come to London? Lucas and I are flying out on Sunday night to see the agent of this actress. Come along if you want. We could have some fun." He took a hand from the wheel and reached for hers.

Anitra drew her hand away and busied herself finding her lipstick and a small mirror in her purse. She concentrated on touching up her mouth. "I don't think so, Lee." She drew neat outlines with a tiny brush. "And don't pretend you'll miss me. Shacking up was fun, wasn't it? But I guess once was enough." She snapped her purse shut and turned to look at him coldly. "Right?"

He drew his shoulders up like a man in a hailstorm. "Whatever you say," he said patiently.

Gary came home that night in a mellow frame of mind. One of the agencies had been saying goodbye to a retiring account supervisor and good old Smitty had invited the representative of his favorite engraving house to stay for a drink. Gary let himself in at seven o'clock and was genuinely surprised to find Anitra in the living room with an empty salad plate beside her, a wine glass in her hand, and a news analysis program on television with the sound turned off. "Hello," he said. "No editing tonight? No answerprints? No emergency at the lab?" He said this without malice.

"You sound happy."

"We just put Elgar Smith out to pasture. They made nice advertising men in those days."

"There's a salad plate for you in the fridge."

"Thanks." His smile was that of a man who's been told his lottery ticket is a winner for the third consecutive week. He came back from the kitchen with his plate and a wine glass. Anitra poured Riesling for him as he peeled off the cling-film. "Hey, you made tuna with onions" He began eating hungrily.

Anitra reached forward and switched off the TV picture. "What's the word on your film idea?" she asked.

"Early days. I suppose Pennington's working on the treatment."

She set the glass down dead center on a coaster on the broad arm of the sofa. "Luke Pennington has delivered a thirty-page outline to Lee Cosford. They're very excited about it. They have an appointment with an agent in London for next Monday."

Gary beamed and raised his glass. "Fabulous. Thanks for telling me."

"You might well thank me. I don't think Lee was going to mention it." When her husband went on eating, she said, "I saw the script. Your name isn't on it."

"So?"

"So Lee Cosford is running away with your idea, Gary. He fobbed you off on Pennington to get rid of you, and now that Luke says the idea's solid gold, Lee has adopted it."

"That's what I wanted."

"I don't believe this. Lee told me he's going to write you a check once the financing is arranged."

"All donations gratefully received." Gary looked closely at his wife and for the first time saw the extent of her rage. "It's what I wanted," he repeated. "A film about Mama Cass--something to really do her justice. The idea hit me in London when I was walking at night, as if she was still there, her spirit...I know that sounds stupid. But an idea is something from your soul, isn't it? That's all it is and who knows what makes the idea spring into your mind?"

"Gary, come down to earth."

"The film is all that matters. If it's going to be done, I'm delighted. No big deal if my name isn't connected with it."

"But it's your concept, damn it! You've got to be credited! Call a lawyer tomorrow and explain what's happening. Have a stop put on Lee before he goes any further." Her husband's satisfied face enraged her. "At least get mad! They're ripping you off, they're treating you like a retarded child."

"I can't get mad. I'm too happy."

Anitra picked up the wine bottle but her hands were shaking so hard she could not pour. Her empty glass toppled over. She left it rolling on the carpet. Gary was staring at her now, one cheek full. "Then maybe you'll get mad at this," she said. "While you were over in London falling in love with the ghost of Cass Elliott, I was back here in bed with Lee Cosford. Yes, that's right." She got up and said over her shoulder as she left the room, "Now will you come back into this world, Gary?"

Anitra found it easy to make her decision the next day. Her mind was influenced by the way the men around her seemed determined to conduct business as usual. Gary did his typical early-morning flit to work, leaving one of his screwy notes on the kitchen counter. Years ago he had played with the idea of being a cartoonist; now the talent had mostly evaporated, leaving a residue of doodled heads and neat printing. Today's note referred only obliquely to last night in a speech balloon that said, "Don't blame yourself. We'll talk."

At the studio, Cosford scurried around in his characterization as Laughing Lee the benign executive. He had everybody around the place grinning, but the best Anitra could give him was a sour, knowing smile. His only direct communication with her was when he whipped into her office and said, "Do me a favor, will you, Anitra?

Stephie is away sick or I'd ask her. Drive the car around to the garage and have them check the steering. Tell him about the shudder around ninety. And I'll need it by Sunday."

"I'll call and see if they can do it now," Anitra said curtly. She picked up the phone and dialed for an outside line. But when Lee left the office she set the phone down again without making the call. The suggestion in her mind was unthinkable, but she had to consider it. She did so and came to the conclusion that Cosford had something coming. Not that an accident would happen. But if it did there would be justice in it.

Later, Cosford had to go to a luncheon meeting at the Queen Elizabeth Hotel, so he took a taxi. He telephoned from there to say that he was accepting a lift with his dairy client down to the farm in the Eastern Townships. He would be there for the weekend, returning Sunday at midday to get the car and the film scenario from his office and then to drive Luke Pennington to the airport. Would Anitra be able to come in for an hour on Sunday to discuss taking over the reins during his absence?

"Of course." She pursued her curt manner, words at a premium. "They kept the car at the garage but promised the steering will be fixed by Saturday afternoon. I'll see that it's here."

"You're a gem." Lee was expansive after his lunch. "I'll bring you back something nice from Bond Street."

On Sunday morning as Anitra was leaving for the studio, Gary came out of the guest room where he had been sleeping for a couple of nights. "Have you got a minute to talk?" he said.

"I'm in a hurry."

"I've decided you're right, I'm going to see a lawyer next week. As long as the film is being made, I might as well get some credit."

He was not looking directly at her, so she was able to observe the veiled look on his face. "You still aren't mad, Gary. You're just saying what you think I want to hear."

His voice became petulant. "Well, how the hell am I supposed to please you?"

"Nobody's asking you for that. Just grow up. When somebody walks all over you, be a man—get mad."

He followed her to the door. "Are you going to see Lee?"

"I'm going to the studio. There's work to be done before he leaves for London."

When she was gone, Gary went into the living room and pressed the palms of his hands together. He looked around. Nothing like Sunday morning light to show the dust on everything. Anitra liked to go about with a spray can and a cloth, making everything shine and smell of lemon. Lately there had been other things on her mind.

He took down the most-played cassette in his collection and slipped it into the tape deck. He turned on the amplifier, pressed START, heard a moment's silence and then the familiar harmony flowing from the speakers on the top shelf on either side of the fireplace—Mama Cass's huge, pure voice soaring over the others like a silver-belled horn.

At last he understood why Anitra was angry with him. It was a matter of expressing himself as unselfconsciously as the beautiful, natural woman he was listening to. Gary knew how he felt; he had to tell Lee Cosford how he felt.

By one o'clock, Anitra had made two big drinks each for Cosford and Pennington. She had poured on the whiskey for her boss and stinted the ginger. He was rolling with self-importance. She was glad when he looked at his watch.

"Time to hit the road," he said. "Where's the car, Anitra?"

"Around back." She had moved it there herself on Saturday. "The guy from the garage couldn't find any place else to park."

"Then we're off. Come on, young Lucas—Daddy is going to show you the world. So long, Mrs. Prime."

When the door closed behind them Anitra poured herself a small drink and took it to Lee's desk where she sat down and rummaged till she found a copy of the Mama Cass scenario. Then she began to sip and read. As she turned the pages the realization dawned on her that this would make a great film. Gary was dead right. If things worked out, she and he would take it to another producer and have a go themselves.

●　●　●　●

Lee Cosford drove aggressively to the corner and stamped on the brake pedal, throwing Pennington forward so that he had to catch himself against the padded dashboard.

"Ride 'em, cowboy," Lucas said.

"Haven't lost a passenger in years." Cosford craned his neck. "Isn't that Gary Prime?"

"It sure looks like him."

"Roll your window down. Call him over."

"Are you sure? We don't need him at the moment."

"It's Sunday—I'm feeling Christian. Call him."

Gary saw the face at the car window, wandered over, and bent himself to look inside. "Hello, Lee. I was coming to see you."

"I'm glad. I've been meaning to talk to you about your film. We're just off to the airport. Can you drive out with us and have a drink in the lounge? Don't hesitate, my boy—it's to your benefit. Get in."

As Gary went to open the back door, Lee whispered quickly to Pennington, "Let's give the guy a small credit and one or two percent. It's little enough and may save us litigation later on."

By two-thirty, Anitra had read the script twice and finished a second drink. When the telephone rang, she jumped. It was a police officer. There had been a crash on the highway near Dorval Airport. A car left the road and ran at top speed into a concrete abutment. The license number had been put through the computer which printed out Lee Cosford Productions as owner of the car.

"That was my boss," Anitra said, sounding disturbed. "He was on his way to catch a plane. Is there any --"

"I'm sorry. He must have been going ninety. We haven't been able to get into the car yet, but there can't be anybody alive."

Anitra telephoned him but Gary was either out or not answering. She drove from downtown in twenty minutes, thinking about the accident she had programmed. If it wasn't murder it was certainly manslaughter. Not that Lee or Pennington were any great loss to the world, but she had better not let on to Gary that she had sent her boss out with two doubles on an empty stomach and with faulty steering. Gary lacked the imagination to do anything but call the police.

The apartment was empty. Anitra checked the TV guide and saw that the Expos were on Channel Six in a doubleheader against the Phillies. That meant Gary would be down at the Mount Royal in the television lounge, drinking beer and eating peanuts. No supper required tonight. But perhaps they could have that talk he'd suggested this morning. No need for lawyers now—no bitterness, but a fresh start with an exciting project they could share.

The reaction set in as Anitra made tea. She was trembling so much as she carried it into the living room that she arrived with a brimming saucer. She set it down with both hands, went to turn on the radio, and noticed a cassette inside the deck. She pressed the proper switches and out came the voice Gary had been raving about for the past few weeks, the cause of all the excitement and the manoeuvering and of her deadly intervention.

Now, as never before, she could understand what turned her husband on when this woman sang. Mama Cass was solo on this track, so vibrant and alive she might have been here in the room.

Anitra listened to the entire cassette—both sides—before she realized she was feeling impatient for Gary's return. She began willing him to abandon his precious baseball telecast and get in touch with her. And so when the telephone rang she ran to answer it eagerly.

The Prize in the Pack

Originally published in *Ellery Queen Mystery Magazine*, October 1986.

HERE WAS CASEY DOLAN TRYING TO PREPARE HIS SIX O'CLOCK sports broadcast and there was Carmen's big brother Alvin, waiting for her to finish work and giving Dolan the evil eye from the outer office.

Clement Foy's sonorous voice poured out of the monitor speaker. "A reminder that in fifteen minutes the old catcher will be along with your early-evening sports show. In the meantime, more rolling-home music here on CBAY, the voice of Baytown, as Les Brown and the Band of Renown offer some musical reassurance, 'I've Got My Love To Keep Me Warm.' "

Foy was stuck in the big-band era, which Dolan could stand. At forty-eight, he was five years older than the program director and he liked the bouncy sound. His two-finger typing of tonight's script rattled along almost in time with the rhythm. The age problem, if he had one, was in relation to Carmen Hopkins, who was only nineteen. This was a gap that had seemed unbridgeable six months ago when she came on staff. Now that they had made love, there turned out to be no gap. Dolan had been surprised and gratified but soon learned he was exchanging the fear of inadequacy for that of an early death at the hands of big brother Alvin. He had always suspected there was a trace of Indian in the Hopkins genetic pool. Now those Iroquois eyes watched him from beyond the front desk. Did Alvin know? How could he know? Should Dolan give him a smile?

"I'm on my way," Carmen said, leaving her desk at the back of the room, passing Dolan's chair, letting her fingers brush the back of his neck. "Any problems with continuity, talk to my lawyer." That was a laugh. In six months, she had mastered the job better than anybody the radio station had ever employed. She was good. Too good for such routine work, Dolan kept telling her. "You take it easy now, young lady," he said in an avuncular tone. It was the voice he had used when he was catching for the Redmen and a young pitcher needed reassurance out there on the mound.

"I always try," she said, riveting him with her mischievous stare, "though I don't always succeed." She swaggered away to join her brother. Dolan feasted his eyes on her. She still carried some babyfat he had discovered. Heart-shaped face, lips a bit on the heavy side but perfectly shaped, cheeks forever blushing. Her hair was glossy toffee, tied in twin braids with green ribbons. She had skin that drove Dolan mad, arms, legs, shoulders—she was packaged in this slightly textured, almost café-au-lait material and keeping his hands off it was for the over-the-hill but lately reborn athlete a severe exercise in self-discipline.

"Let's go, Carmen," Alvin said as he opened the door, towering over her, pretending to be out of patience with her instead of her slave, as even Dolan with his deteriorating vision could see. "I want to pick up some beer before the store closes."

"If you're getting drunk tonight," she said, "I'm going out."

Dolan got the message and the typewriter keys jammed. His heart was still pounding like a teenager's when he went on the air ten minutes later. "Good evening, sports fans. First place changed hands last night in the Baytown Fastball League as—"

After he signed off, Dolan drove home and showered and washed what was left of his hair. He was still using Anna's shampoo. A few drops was all he needed, so three months after his wife's departure for Centralia the big plastic bottle was holding out. The smell still reminded him of her. So did the bath itself, oddly and sadly. In early years, when David was still a baby, they sometimes performed what seemed in those days an adventurous act—they got into the shower together. Soaping each other, they laughed a lot and he called her his seal. Now—it seemed no more than a few weeks later—David was in charge of the science department at Centralia Polytechnic while his mother had opened a shop in the same city selling coordinated paints and wallpapers. And Dad was making it on his own.

Dolan rubbed himself dry with a rough towel. He faced the mirror at an angle that showed the least paunch, the fewest veins. Carmen seemed to like him. Mind you, it was always lights off and after a couple of drinks. He got dressed in the coordinated green-and-grey outfit, a modified track suit. The store manager had said he looked twenty years younger. Anna would laugh. She had forever been after Dolan to smarten himself up, buy new clothes. All she had to do to get her wish was leave him.

She hasn't really left me, Dolan said to himself as he pocketed money and keys and went outside into a balmy summer night. After twenty-six years together, we're trying it apart. A little freedom, room to move.

He knew he'd find Carmen in the back lounge of the Coronet Hotel. It was her idea to conduct their meetings in the public eye. "If we sneak around and drive out to The Cedars like you're suggesting, somebody is bound to see us and say those two are up to something. But here in the heart of town, how bad can it be? We're fellow employees having a drink together."

"My problem will be keeping my hands off you," he said.

"I have the cure. Think of you touching me, and then Alvin walking in."

The blind jazz pianist was at the keyboard when Dolan entered the lounge. His dog lay at his feet, head down, barely tolerant of what was going on. Jack Danforth, owner of the Coronet, sat at the end of the bar. Dolan placed himself at a corner table, distributed a few waves, and ordered a large brandy-and-soda. He was halfway through it when Carmen appeared, spotted him, hugged the wall on her way to the table, and slipped furtively onto a chair.

"Are you all right?" he asked her.

"Do I look all right?"

He studied her face. It might have been called a swelling on the jaw. "There's no light in here. Have you been hit?"

The music climaxed, lots of applause, end of set. Pianist and see-ing-eye dog filed out behind Danforth to sit in his office. Carmen was at her most rebellious, a sailor on leave. "I came so close to put-ting a knife in him, Casey—"

"Tell me."

"It's one thing when he nags me. That's what a big brother is for. But when he started in on Peter, I went for him."

"Calm down."

"All right. All right. Get me a beer."

He ordered a Molson and another brandy. The drinks came and they started in on them but she was still taking deep breaths through her nostrils. In this mood, she was more attractive than ever to Dolan.

"Did he know you were coming out to meet me?"

"No. I don't know. I don't care. Do you care?"

"I don't care."

"Stop worrying about my brother. I'm over eighteen, I can do whatever I want. There's not a damn thing Alvin can do about it."

Dolan tried to put from his mind thoughts of Alvin Hopkins doing something about it and then being punished for it by a life sentence, with Dolan no longer around to appreciate justice being done. "What made you so mad?" he asked.

"He said I'm not a responsible person. Without him to look after me, I'd go down the drain. He thinks I should still be at university."

Dolan thought so, too, but knew better than to tell the head-strong girl. She was a classic under-achiever. Born with brains to spare and limitless energy, she refused ever to do more than just enough to get by. In Baytown High School, she got top grades while hardly cracking a book. Her brother Alvin, with no encouragement from Carmen, borrowed the money to pay for her first year in an arts course at Queen's University in Kingston, sixty miles down the road, past Centralia. He bullied her into registering and moving there and attending some lectures. But she only stayed three weeks, arriving back home on the bus, her trunk showing up, rail freight, a few days later.

The debacle cost Alvin a good part of the money he paid. And when his clever little sister got a job selling dresses at Artistic Ladies

Wear, it was almost more than he could bear. The new job writing continuity (whatever that was) at CBAY was an improvement. But still she seemed more interested in going through the motions and having fun than in getting ahead. For a man who used all his limited ability to work his way up through the yards to a job behind a ticket window at the CN station, Carmen's behavior was calculated to drive him up the wall.

Dolan said to her, "What did he say about Pete?" Carmen Hopkins' other brother Peter, known to his friends as Hophead, had killed himself two years ago in a road accident involving his pickup truck and a steel power pylon.

"He said I'm not just bad for myself, I'm a bad influence on other people. That's a laugh. Pete was drunk when he showed up that night."

"I know."

"I couldn't ask him to stay. It was a girls' party. And he kept grabbing hold of people, it wasn't funny. Vera didn't like him and he kept grabbing hold of Vera."

Dolan had heard the story before. "So you ordered him out," he said gloomily.

"I whacked him and pushed him out the door and locked it. Then when I went after him, it was too late. He was driving away."

Dolan stared into the battered-baby eyes, hoping it was over. "Carmen," he said softly, "it was not your fault."

After a minute or so, she became calm. "You've had a normal life, eh, Case?" she said. "Good family. Lots of success."

"Yeah, sure." He gave her the grin that usually worked. "The only reason the Redmen kept old Casey Dolan behind the plate was I didn't mind being hit by bouncing baseballs." He took a drink. "And with our pitching we had a lot of bouncing baseballs." He showed her his collection of broken fingers.

"It's a wonder you can type," she said.

"It explains a lot," he said.

They went off for a drive later, across the Bay Bridge and into the county. The windows were down and there was a lot of clover in the air. On the radio, Clem Foy was doing his night show, ignoring the musical tastes of his audience, playing a selection of 78s from his own library. He thanked Lionel Hampton for rendering "Midnight Sun," then introduced Louie singing "A Kiss To Build a Dream On."

As they approached the colored lights of a roadhouse, Carmen said she was hungry. Dolan drove in and parked in darkness on the farthest patch of gravel and went inside to get takeaway, leaving her in the car.

"That really cheeses me off," she said when he came back with hamburgers and shakes. He could feel the vibrations, so he switched on and got rolling again, heading farther into farmland. "You won't even take me inside," she complained with her mouth full. "I feel like some kind of cheap whore."

Half an hour later, he parked off the road on a headland with a view of the bay where it becomes part of Lake Ontario. Her mood was sweet again. Dolan kissed her, and his advancing years faded, leaving him feeling strong, not worried for the moment about anything. He knew it was only nature trying to get him to propagate the race, but he didn't care. Her mouth was soft, she smelled of soap and lipstick.

On the way home, she was buoyant. Her window was down, her eyes narrowed against the rush of air. "If you and I were married, there'd be no problem," she said. "Alvin would have to shut up."

"I'm already married. Did you forget?"

"She's left you. Get a divorce."

"What's the rush to get married? You're a kid, you've got your whole life. You're a talented girl, you can write up a storm. I'm just a stupid ball player but I can recognize what you've got."

"Here we go."

"You sit at that desk bashing out promotion announcements and program scripts with one brain tied behind your back. Work, damn it. Write." He glanced at her face, saw the down-turned mouth. "Develop the talent God gave you."

"Who asked Him?" she said. Then after half a mile of slipstream, she said, "Would you marry me if I said I was pregnant?   I'm not, but if I told you I was?" She was smiling now. "You wouldn't believe me, would you?"

"Not in the nineteen-eighties." He shrugged. "I believed it in the fifties."

* * * *

Carmen passed Dolan's desk one afternoon in the following week and dropped a sheaf of folded typewritten pages in front of him. "Read it and weep," she said and wandered away. He glanced at page one, saw "Nor Iron Bars by Carmen Hopkins." He was so excited by the manuscript, he couldn't get on with his work. He took it to the washroom and read it in the privacy of a cubicle.

She had written a story about a young girl in love with an older man. They both worked in a small-town radio station. There was practically no invention in it, the plot was his experience and hers, but it read like a house afire. At the end, the sports announcer was still with his wife and the girl was floating face-down in the bay.

He emerged into the office and went to her desk, where she was elaborately turning the pages of a newspaper. "Come for coffee," he said, handing her the manuscript.

"You like?" It was the only time she had appeared nervous in front of him.

"Come for coffee."

They went around the corner to the Paragon Cafe, where he ordered two coffees and the slab of cream pie she asked for. A kid. "Your story is brilliant," he said. "Exactly what I wanted you to do. Keep it up."

"What for?"

"Because you can."

"I tried it and now I know how easy it is. Big deal."

"You want to be infuriating, don't you? Who are you trying to provoke, your father?"

"The great prospector?" She laughed. "All he ever did was search for uranium that wasn't there and come back once in a while to get my mother pregnant."

"Succeed for yourself," Dolan pontificated. "Not for anybody else."

Carmen finished her pie, gave him the mischievous smile with her mouth half full. "I forget," she said. "Did you promise the other night to marry me if you got me pregnant?"

He knew she was teasing him, but his heart turned over anyway. "One of these days, kid—over my knee."

"Ready when you are," she said.

*　*　*　*

The Redmen were batting in the bottom of the third against the Napanee Oilers. The sun was setting behind the canning factory. Seated at the microphone in the press box under the grandstand roof, Dolan called the balls and strikes and kept up a flow of anecdote and description. He was feeling at peace with the world, almost smug, hoping Management never discovered that he would broadcast baseball for nothing. In the bleachers, several hundred fans in shirtsleeves watched and ate and drank and yelled at the players and the umpires.

Around eight o'clock, Carmen made her way up the ladder and took a seat not far from Dolan. Perhaps to make her entry legal, she had put on her CBAY T-shirt. She was munching caramel corn from the famous narrow red box. When they cut back to the studio for a commercial she extended the package in his direction.

"Thanks, I can't. Gets in my throat."

"Is it all right for me to be here?"

He looked at the scrubbed healthy face, the glistening braids, the ripe body in a shirt one size too small. "It is absolutely perfect for you to be here." Then, encouraged by her glow, and just before his cue from the engineer, he said to her, "Carmen dear, life is a box of Cracker Jack and you are the prize in the pack."

She stirred the air above her head with a finger. "Hoopdedoo!" she said.

After the game, they walked to his car in the parking lot behind the dance pavilion. The Clem Foy Five was playing inside, and through screened windows colored lights glowed behind the movement of dancing couples. They watched in silence holding hands. It was a big regret for Dolan that he couldn't take the girl inside and hold her for a while to music. Now he drew her to him. She must have been reading his mind because she angled her cheek against his shoulder, rested her hand on his collar, pressed herself against him, and moving hardly at all, unsteady on gravel, they danced part of a chorus of "Moonglow."

"Come here often?" she said to lighten the atmosphere. He said nothing, unlocked the car, let her in, slammed the door, and strode around to the driver's side. As he switched on, backed away, gunned a ferocious turn, and raced out of the fair grounds, she said, "You can come home with me tonight."

He said, "What?"

"Alvin has gone away for few days. A friend of his called and asked him to go up to Montreal for some stag thing. A guy they know is getting married. He got on the train this afternoon."

Dolan drove in silence.

"On the other hand, if you don't want to—I just thought it would be nice to get in bed and not have to worry about rushing off."

He thought of what she had written. The young girl dead by her own hand. The possessive brother. The old athlete trying to squeeze a few more drops of flavor out of a desiccated life. She called it Nor Iron Bars. "I want to," he said as he made the turn to take them down the hill toward Station Street. "I just can't believe my luck." In his mind, cutting through the confusion, Dolan heard a sound that was not hard to identify. It was the door of a cage slamming shut behind him...

Her house reminded Dolan of vacation cottages he had inhabited in wilderness country. It was of frame construction, ramshackle, okay in summer as long as it didn't rain. The furnishings were lightweight, carpets worn through, woodwork covered in paint faded years since to the color of an ancient keyboard. The telephone (only once had Dolan dared speak to her on this vulnerable line) hung on the kitchen wall. For a yard around it, the wallpaper was peppered with a buckshot explosion of scrawled numbers and messages.

She found a bottle of gin and gave him a drink he did not want. "Relax," she said, bouncing into place beside him on the sprung settee, tucking a leg under her where he could not miss seeing the plump, shiny curve where calf met thigh.

She surveyed him with delight. "You're among friends, Casey. Don't look so mournful."

She gave him butterfly kisses with her eyelashes. He let his hand rest on that smooth leg. His anxiety evaporated and he began to share her excitement. The feeling reminded him of a time when he and some of the kids went into Woolworth's on Front Street and lifted a few lead soldiers. It was wrong and he knew he would hate himself later, but the urge had been irresistible.

Her bedroom was through a curtained doorway off the sitting room. She said, "Give me a minute," and went in there. Dolan sat, glass in both hands, elbows on knees, staring at the floor. Strange, he thought. The room smelled of decay, it showed no evidence of maintenance and yet he sensed there was a stability about the place as if it would still be here, sheltering the Hopkins tribe in a hundred years, long after his tidy bungalow had been bulldozed and built over.

"Ready!"

He went to her in the silent bedroom, saw a small cot with the covers turned back, inviting in pink light from a tiny lamp. She was naked under a flimsy gown, torn at the hip. He embraced her and was so overpowered that he lost his balance and they did a struggling dance, laughing at themselves. "You'd better lie down," she said, "before you fall down."

The front door opened, then closed with a slam. Alvin's voice was bored. "Carmen? You home?"

Dolan went ice cold. He stepped away from her and faced the curtain. Footsteps in the other room. The brother's boots showed in the light at the hem of the curtain. "You decent, kid?"

"Yes," she said in a tone of great weariness.

"What is it?"

"You may as well come in."

Alvin drew the curtain aside. He saw Dolan, saw his sister sitting on the edge of the bed. "What the hell?" He stayed where he was but raised his arm and pointed a finger at Dolan's face. "You bastard!"

"Alvin, calm down. He's here because I asked him. I work, I bring in money—"

"Shut your mouth."

"You don't own me!"

"Shut up!" Alvin's voice rose. He moved toward Dolan.

"Listen! Listen to me!" Carmen ran at her brother, grabbed his arm, and used her strength to turn him. "You touch him, you lay a hand on him—" her finger was in his face now "—and I'll be gone so far from here you'll never see me again!"

Dolan felt as if he had been tied hand and foot and set on fire. He was due to die horribly and could do nothing about it. Shock numbed him. "I don't want any trouble," he said lamely, able to feel embarrassment through his panic at the weakness of his response.

"Just go, Casey." Carmen put her back against her brother, making way for Dolan's departure. "Don't say anything, get out, I'll take care of this." As he fled, she told him, "I'll talk to you tomorrow."

Seated in his car where he had parked it on the next street, Dolan had to wait a good minute before his fingers could fit the key to the ignition lock. As he drove away, he assured himself of one good thing emerging from the debacle—he would certainly not be spending any more time with that dangerous little bitch.

Carmen was waiting for Dolan in the Coronet lounge. She had telephoned in sick to the radio station, taking a day's leave. At four in the afternoon, with his evening broadcast mostly prepared, he had responded to her call and come down to see her. She was halfway through a beer. Soon due on the air, Dolan ordered coffee.

"Can you believe it?" she opened. "That whole business about the stag in Montreal was a put-on. He suspected us. He set it up to catch you with me."

Dolan could believe anything of Alvin and he said so.

"You don't have to worry," she said. "I'm sorry I put you through it."

"Not your fault," he said bleakly. But he thought it was—why couldn't she just leave him alone? He was old enough to be her father. Why all the provocative attention?

"We talked for a long time after you left. Alvin can be sweet when you approach him the right way. At first he didn't want to know but I kept on and finally he understood. We love each other."

"Carmen, did you see his face?"

"He was all right later. I told him you want to marry me."

"Carmen—"

"Don't you? Are you just in this for what you can get?"

"You know better."

"Well?"

He tried to be patient with this stubborn child. "I have a wife."

"You talk as if you've got cancer. Millions of men get cured of wives. It's called divorce."

"It takes two to get a divorce."

"Have you asked her? She doesn't even live with you. She's over in Centralia having a ball running her store. She's probably waiting for you to bring up the subject."

It was all so complicated. What had happened to the quiet life he used to think was boring? A divorce would cost money. A wedding would cost money. Carmen would get pregnant. Babies cost money. He would be the oldest daddy in Baytown—laughter in the beverage rooms, to say the least.

He drank his coffee doggedly, aware that she was watching him across her beer.

"Okay," he said at last. "I'll drive over to Centralia and put the question to her."

Dolan waited until Sunday when he had no program to do and then drove down the Bayshore Road through a region of dairy farms and acres of half-grown corn, reaching the concrete towers of Centralia at five o'clock in the afternoon.

He had always hated the big city. Years ago, the Redmen had come up against Centralia in a sudden-death semifinal leading to the Southern Ontario Baseball League championship. Baytown lost the game eleven to four and Dolan, besides going hitless, had allowed the ball to get past him twice and each time a run scored while he was scrambling around twenty feet behind home-plate, trying to find the handle.

Warned by his telephone call the day before, Anna was waiting for him in the back garden when he walked around the side of the house. It was bigger than his place back home but she was only renting it, furnished. Reclining in a folding chair, an empty one beside her, she raised her sunglasses and studied him as he shambled across the grass.

"You've lost weight," she said.

"Pining away without you."

"You look younger." Her voice and her frown conveyed suspicion. "What's her name?"

There was a pitcher of lemonade and a couple of glasses on a table between the chairs. He poured himself a splash and sat down. "You're a mindreader."

"Why else would you ask to come and see me?"

"Maybe I miss you."

"Maybe, but you don't." She had not taken her eyes from his face. "Don't look so pathetic. I wrote us off a long time ago."

"I hate it when you say that."

"Stop clinging to a finished thing. Move on, Case."

He set down his empty glass on the tin table. It rang like the signal for the start of round one. "Funny you should say that, Annie. I need a divorce."

"So. What's her name?"

"Carmen Hopkins."

Anna turned her head.

"Is that the fat little teenager I met the last time I came into the station? You must be joking."

"She's a clever young woman."

"She's a bloody genius if she's trapped you." Her face was pale, she looked her age. "Is she pregnant?"

"Not that I've heard."

"She's saving her trump card. Casey, listen to me, I'm about to do you a favor."

"I'm listening."

"No way will I ever grant you a divorce to marry that carnivorous high-school dropout. If you were to come to me with some mature, intelligent, decent woman —" She watched his face for a few minutes while he counted blooms on hollyhocks. Then she got up and carried the pitcher and her glass to the house. "Crazy," she threw back at him. "Out of sight."

Dolan came in a few minutes later and heard the shower drumming. He wandered through rooms he had seen only once before. He used to believe, like a kid, that he and Anna in the house in Baytown were permanent because nothing else could ever contain their relationship. He was wrong. There was always another way.

She joined him as he was exploring the bedroom. It was a new robe, soft towelling in a shade of blue he liked, and she smelled of the lilac soap she had brought into his life decades ago. She stood beside him; there was no place for his arm except across her hip. They slipped easily into a familiar embrace. As they kissed, she whispered, "I was hoping you hadn't driven all this way just to argue."

"Seems I didn't," he said.

In the next hour, the light in the room diminished slowly as afternoon became evening. Casey lay at ease with Anna tucked close against his side. The occasional things she said buzzed against his ear. He was falling asleep. The trip had solved nothing. All it proved was that he and Anna could still get it on, but that had never been in doubt. They could not live together, and she would never, clearly, release him to marry Carmen.

"No divorce?"

"No divorce."

"You're a bitch," he said.

"I'm the best friend you ever had."

They ate something at nine o'clock. By then, he was outside unlocking the car, making his escape from boredom, the nagging that was beginning to emerge—not all hers, he was dishing out his share. The car smelled strange inside, but he cranked down the window, switched on, and began to roll. Then Alvin Hopkins got up off the floor behind the driver's seat and put a knife against his neck.

"Hey!" The car swerved before Casey got control and stepped on the brake, easing to a stop fifty yards from Anna's house.

"Keep driving."

"How the hell did you get in here?"

"You shouldn't have given Carmen your spare key. She doesn't even have a license."

"She told me she does."

"She tells you lots of things. Like I was going to Montreal for a friend's wedding."

"She made that up?'

"That's right. My sister is crazy, don't you know that? After Pete crashed his truck and died, she went out of the house one night and put her head on the mainline track, waiting for the Toronto express. I think she knew I'd find her and bring her back but I'm not sure."

"So the whole story about she'd be alone in the house for a couple of days was to get me found there by you."

"She likes excitement."

They drove slowly in silence, down empty streets. At last Dolan said, "Where are we going?"

"I'm going back to Baytown. By bus, the way I came."

Dolan felt, at last, the cold tide of fear. It filled his gut, loosened his muscles, his foot relaxed on the accelerator.

"Don't do anything crazy."

"Keep driving. Turn left at the corner."

They drove into an area with trees and shrubs on either side of the road. Streetlamps cast pools of brilliance which only emphasized the black distances beyond.

"Slow down. Pull off over there, between the lights. Here."

Dolan switched off and sat, trembling, sweating ice-water. "If you want me to stay away from Carmen, you've got it. I was just with my wife—we're planning on getting back together."

"It's Carmen staying away from you. She'll never do it, no matter what I tell her. She's a bad little girl. It's vital that I prevent her having her own way. The kid is spoiled rotten." Alvin leaned forward. "Now look at this. I want you to see something." He held the knife blade in front of Dolan's face. The thick fist, the muscular wrist formed an unbreakable grip that trembled slightly. The blade itself gleamed—at least seven inches long, a streak of oil on the honed edge. "If you yell. If you run. If you do anything but as I say, this goes into your gut and I turn it."

"Oh, Jesus," Dolan whimpered."Jesus."

"Get out of the car. Slowly."

Hopkins was out and waiting for him on the pavement, took his arm as he slammed the door and led the old ballplayer away from the light and down a pathway smelling of ripe earth. Furtive movement occurred at intervals in the shadows. "This is where the Gays hang out," Alvin said. "We're not alone."

They came to a silent clearing. Dolan could make out the surroundings, could see the shape of Alvin Hopkins as he was forced around to face him. "You'll be robbed and stabbed a lot. They have these crazy killings here all the time. But you've behaved, so I'm not going to hurt you. This blade is razor-sharp. I'll cut your throat—you won't even feel it. Then I'll do the rest. Believe me, it won't hurt."

Casey Dolan found the desperate courage to raise his voice "Not going to hurt me?" he screamed. "Bloody hell, you're killing me!"

Alvin moved swiftly, turned Dolan, lifted his chin, and swung the knife. And he was right about that important thing—Dolan didn't even feel it.

Six months passed, during which Carmen Hopkins stayed late every night at the radio station. She told her brother she was writing a novel. He didn't believe her, he thought she was messing around with Dolan's replacement. But try as he would, however often he popped in unexpectedly, he always found her at the old typewriter, knocking hell out of the keys.

Then it was finished and she began coming home after work, eating whatever he put in front of her, then watching television until signoff. It was agreeable in a way, a nice routine which Alvin appreciated. But she was putting on weight and had stopped doing anything with her hair, which gave him an uneasy feeling. In fact, by the end of the year she was looking more like a fat sloven than his sexy little sister.

"You should take a look at yourself in the mirror," he said to her one evening.

"You should burn in hell," was her calm response.

The letter from Toronto came one Saturday morning while Carmen was still in bed. She received little mail, but whatever arrived with her name on it, Alvin opened and read. This one was first-class, typewritten envelope, a company name in the corner— Tandem Publishing Ltd. The letter was brief. It said:

"Dear Miss Hopkins:

Thank you for letting us see your novel, Hey, Don't You Remember? It needs a bit of tightening but it is a powerful work and we would like to publish it. Is it autobiographical? The character of the psychopathic brother, Al, is particularly well drawn, while the doomed love affair between the young girl and the broadcaster is poignant, to say the least.

Can you come to Toronto and talk to us? I'll look forward to an early reply—"

Holding letter and envelope in one hand, Alvin shuffled across the room in his broken slippers, drew back the curtain, and went through into the musty cave where Carmen lay asleep on her cot. She was breathing slowly, a hand resting below her chin, wrinkled thumb not far from her open mouth. When it used to be his job to watch her as a child, Alvin had repeatedly dragged the wet thumb free, trying to break her of the habit. Another failure.

Now he had a new problem. His little sister was going to become a published author. She would be rich and famous and a guest on TV chat shows, where she would discuss the background of her book. Or not. It was up to him and he would have to make up his mind soon.

Counting her shallow breaths, eyeing the pillow on the floor beside the cot, Alvin smiled with deep affection. "Carmen, Carmen," he said softly, "What in the world am I going to do with you?"

Silently, in the Dead of Night

Originally published in *Ellery Queen Mystery Magazine*, January 1984.

THE TELEPHONE RANG ON THE BEDSIDE TABLE AND JARRED Birtles awake. He picked it up and listened.

"Norman?"

"What time is it?" The dryness in his mouth was not unpleasant. He had taken just the right amount of whisky but not enough sleep.

"Almost eight. I thought you'd be up."

"I don't go in till one. Charlie opens the place today." He stared at the window and the grey autumn light. "It's as if I'm still delivering the mail."

"I'm sorry." But she didn't sound sorry. She sounded as bright as her lacquered hair. Birtles could imagine Anitra Colahan dressed and groomed as for a tango competition, earrings sparkling, short skirt flaring over several crinolines. "I missed you last night," she said. "I thought you were coming over."

"We had trouble balancing the cash after we closed. And then Charlie offered me a lift home." Only partly a lie. The cash had been a problem but he ended up taking a cab from the rank outside Wimbledon Station.

"I would have driven you home."

"I don't want you on the roads at that time of night." What Birtles really didn't want was to be stuck in the death seat speeding along London streets after midnight. Anitra had taken the driving test three times before passing. Her style at the wheel was risky and spectacular, much like her performance on the dance floor.

"Can you come by the studio tonight?" she asked. "I have something to tell you. Something nice."

"O.K. I finish at six."

"Lovely. We can go to the Taj. It's good news, Norman."

Birtles checked the bathroom window-ledge but found no note. When Barbie wanted to be called in the morning, she would leave a page from her notebook pinned under the talcum-powder tin and the breezy words, the erratic left-handed scrawl always gave Birtles a lift. The absence of a note probably meant his daughter would be sleeping till noon. Which meant he wouldn't see her before he went to the poolroom. One more day gone from the diminishing week before she took off for Canada.

Birtles went downstairs and along the hall toward the kitchen, passing Barbie's bedroom on the way. The door was open. What he saw stopped him cold. The room was empty, the backpack gone, her makeup, brush, and comb vanished from the dresser. The bed was in disarray but that was normal—he couldn't tell if she had slept here last night.

Perhaps she'd left a note somewhere in the room. Birtles looked around but found no message among the clutter of pop-music magazines, soft-drink tins, overloaded ashtrays, and the accumulation of discarded clothing.

There was a coffee mug on the bedside table. Birtles picked it up carefully—sometimes they were half full of murky liquid. This one was dry but there was a crumpled envelope tucked inside it.

He unfolded the envelope, found it unaddressed. Some greenish-brown grains of leaf fell into the palm of his hand. They looked like something from one of his spice jars. Printed in the corner of the envelope was: Hotel Candide, Inverness Avenue, London W2.

Carrying his discovery into the kitchen, Birtles put the kettle on, made toast, made coffee, ate and drank standing while he tried to handle his feelings. The sight of Barbie's room deserted had shaken him. He was not looking forward to her going away. When his wife died six years ago, he had kept going, for Barbie's sake. Part of him had wanted to convert what little he had into cash and head off to some hot country where his main duty would have been to keep himself drunk.

Instead, he had become a meal-maker and housekeeper. Well, it was an achievement, something to be proud of, and Barbie's confident character was the result. His example had taught her how to soldier on. Now, apparently, she had packed up her possessions in her old kit bag and hit the long, long trail. Without even saying goodbye.

No, that wasn't possible. Barbie with her curly head and the sweet baby face and her silent understanding of what he was going through in losing her would never do a moonlight flit. Fear hit Birtles in the stomach like a draught of acid. Something had happened to her. She was in trouble.

It was early to ring Jeremy but Birtles couldn't wait. The boy came on the phone coughing like a veteran. "Sorry to disturb you but I was wondering if you saw Barbie last night."

"We didn't, Mr. Birtles. The band was playing at the Ploughman. If she'd been in, I'd have known about it."

"O.K. Sorry to wake you."

"Barbie hasn't come around much the last few months. She's saving her money."

"I know. I've had to put up with her almost every night. Like an old married couple." Birtles kept two trays handy and produced supper regularly in front of the TV. They watched everything, not reacting much, in comforting balance there side by side in the upholstered chairs drawn round to face the screen.

"If you see her, ask her to call home."

At the poolroom, only three of the nineteen tables were in use. It was too nice a day for people to be inside shooting snooker. Charlie was behind the counter serving the occasional beer or Coke, answering the phone, reading a tabloid of few words and many pictures. It was pointless for two of them to be on duty on such a quiet afternoon, so Birtles suggested Charlie take off.

"I'll go in a minute." Charlie went on reading. Birtles strode back and forth, his rangy figure looming large over the counter. When he had been employed by the Post Office, before the economy cuts made him redundant, more than one customer told him they always knew when the mail was on the way, he was so easy to spot coming up the street. Now he mopped clean a spotless surface, snapped his fingers, opened and closed the refrigerator cabinet.

"You're giving me the creeps, Norman. Settle down."

Suddenly, at the end of the room where the card table was situated, a chair was kicked back, players were on their feet, arms extended across the table grabbing shirtfronts. Without a word, Birtles reached for the light panel and snapped the switch controlling the lamp over the table. He raised the counter gate and strode to the scene, head on one side, arms loose, the picture of a man with his patience exhausted. He recognized the troublemaker and faced him.

"You! Out!" Said while pointing at the door.

"This geezer's won all the money and now he wants to quit."

"I said when I sat down I'd have to leave—"

Birtles cut through the argument. "Walk to the door. If I have to say it again, you won't touch many steps on the way down."

Back behind the counter, his hands trembled as he tried to open a box of pool chalk. The cubes went all over the counter, some on the floor. Charlie watched him. "Are you all right?"

"A little nervous."

"You were awfully rough for a first offense."

"A little nervous today."

Charlie folded his paper and took the afternoon off. When he reported back at six, Birtles washed up and then walked on down the Broadway to the dance salon. He climbed more stairs and emerged in the ballroom. Anitra was on the floor with her client, taking him through the basic movements of the cha-cha. As they vamped across acres of polished hardwood, their images were reflected in a series of mirrors.

Birtles took a chair against the wall. The client had the grace of a piano mover but Anitra managed to make him look competent. She glistened in her freshly done peach hair, her swirling skirt, those shiny tapered legs ending in blue sequined high-heeled pumps. "One and two, cha-cha-cha," she commanded while the recording of a brassy Latin band played "Tea For Two." She spotted Birtles and blew him a kiss.

The client left at last after an exchange of money and a flurry of cheek-kissing. Anitra came and sat beside Birtles, kicking off her shoes and slipping into a pair that looked less like they had been built by a custom-car maker. "Bless his heart," she said, "he'll never be a dancer but it keeps me working."

"What's your good news?" Birtles asked, putting on a smile.

"You look tired. Are you all right?"

"You said it was special."

"They're making me manager here. That means I'll get a regular salary in addition to the fees for my lessons."

"Congratulations." She was expecting to be kissed. He leaned towards that rouged cheek, inhaled the lilac scent, kissed her. That was the trouble—she was warm and soft and if he wasn't careful she would become a part of him and then she would leave or die and that part would be torn out without benefit of anaesthetic.

"I think you should let me treat you to dinner," she said.

"Never refuse a free meal."

They went next door to the Taj Mahal and ordered onion bah-jis, Madras curry and chapatis, and a bottle of white wine. Late in the meal, Birtles found the courage to say: "Barbie wasn't there this morning. Her room was empty, everything gone as if she'd moved out. But she'd never do that without telling me."

"I knew something was the matter. When is she supposed to leave for Canada?"

"End of next week."

"No note in her room? Nothing?"

Birtles took the crumpled envelope out of his pocket and put it on the table. "I found this."

"Hotel Candide." Anitra studied the few grains of leaf. "Looks like something the kids smoke."

"I suppose so. They tell me it's no worse than this." He drank some wine. "I'm wondering if it's a clue to where she might have gone. The envelope, I mean."

"Are you thinking of calling the police?"

"They wouldn't want to know. A girl Barbie's age, they'd assume she's gone off with friends. Especially since she's saved up a pile of money and had a trip planned."

"How much has she saved?"

"Over six hundred pounds. It was all in traveller's checks. She was ready to go."

Anitra poured the grains back into the envelope. "Where do you suppose she got this?"

"I'm not sure. There was a girl came to see her the other day but she didn't stay long. A girl from up the hill in the village. Barbie told me her name—Lucy Feather."

Birtles remembered the girl's arrival at the front door one morning a couple of days ago. Barbie was still in bed. "I'm Lucy Feather. Did Barbie tell you I'd be coming by? She has a book I'd like to borrow."

"Yes, she mentioned you. Come in, you may have to wake her up. It's the door at the end of the hall." Birtles watched the movement of her skintight jeans. She was a solid girl with hair three shades of blonde. Her tweed jacket was expensive; she was not one of the dole-queue layabouts who comprised most of Barbie's list of friends.

Birtles went into the kitchen. Through the wall he heard their voices but not their words. The conversation was not exactly amicable. Barbie's final statement sounded like an invitation for Lucy Feather to get the hell out of there.

The bedroom door slammed. Birtles hurried into the hall and accompanied the visitor to the front door. "Got it, thanks." She waved a paperback at him— he recognized it as an in-depth report on a psychopath named Eric Merlot who had drugged and murdered a dozen young travelers in the Far East over a period of years.

When she was gone, Birtles had rapped on Barbie's door and put his head inside the stuffy room.

"Everything O.K.?"

The curly head turned on the pillow and Barbie gave Birtles that reassuring, almost patronizing smile that reminded him of his mother. Who was forty-eight and who was nineteen here? "She wants me to go to India with her instead of Canada. I told her no thanks."

"I heard you."

"All right, I told her to get stuffed. I don't get my kicks from catching dysentery."

"I though she was a friend."

"She's crazy. Her parents threw her out of the house and she came back when they were out and set fire to her room. I can do without friends like her."

Anitra spooned up syrup from her dish of lychees as she listened to Birtles' account of the Lucy Feather visit. At the end, she said: "Is it possible she persuaded Barbie to go with her after all?"

"I doubt it."

"Kids are impulsive. They might have got high last night and decided to head east. Maybe there was a coach leaving late, or somebody with a car. Barbie didn't want to wake you, so she got her stuff and took off. As soon as they come to a phone, she'll get through to you."

"It's a theory. But it doesn't sound like my daughter." Birtles smoothed the envelope and studied the hotel address by the light of the small candle in its red globe.

"All right," Anitra said, "I know what's on your mind. Come on, I'll drive you to Inverness Avenue..."

Thanks to some fine defensive driving by other motorists, Anitra Colahan made the trip safely. She controlled her second-

hand Mini like a rally driver, shoulders up, hands locked on the wheel at the "ten minutes to two" position, and the choreography of her feet on and off the pedals was constant. Birtles braced himself, one hand on the door handle, the other flat against the dash.

"Relax," Anitra said. "Everything's under control."

"Let me out at the traffic lights. I'll get a taxi."

"All right, I'll slow down." She sulked for a few blocks but couldn't contain her aggression any longer than that. Soon she was cutting in and out again, carving up the passive drivers.

Inverness Avenue turned out to be a short street of Edwardian houses not far from Kensington Gardens. Almost without exception, the buildings had been converted into hotels. Anitra found the Candide and parked across the road.

"What do we do now?"

"I'm going to go in and ask a few questions."

"O.K., I'll wait."

"Thanks, but there's no point. If I get no joy from the desk clerk, I'm going to hang around and watch the place."

"More fun for two to watch than one."

"No, really, I'd rather wait alone." He had an idea how to persuade her. He took his key from his pocket and handed it to her. "Go home to my place and wait for me. If Barbie phones like you said, you'll be there to take the message."

He watched the Mini gun down the street and swing abruptly onto Bayswater Road, then he crossed over to the hotel, pushed open the glass door, and went inside. The lobby was simply the former living room with a narrow reception desk added. The rest of the furniture looked like the original pieces. Through a doorway he could see a bar in the adjoining room.

The desk clerk was a young Asian in a pale-blue suit, white shirt, and maroon bow tie. "Sir?"

"I'm looking for a Miss Barbara Birtles. Could you tell me if she's registered?" He spelled the name while the clerk ran down the guest list. When they drew a blank, he asked for Lucy Feather but she wasn't staying at the hotel, either.

"Is it all right if I buy a drink in your bar?"

"We welcome the public, sir."

Birtles went next door, ordered a large whisky, and took it to a seat where he could watch the foot of the staircase in the lobby. His mind began to wander— so far that he almost missed the girl when she appeared. It was the splendid thighs in tight, expensive denim that caught his attention. Lucy Feather was in the lobby, holding out her hand, waiting for someone to come down the stairs and join her.

The companion turned out to be a Eurasian, one of the most handsome men Birtles had ever seen. He was in his early thirties, lean and muscular in white slacks and an open-necked shirt. His black hair swept in a wave across his broad forehead above widely spaced almond eyes.

It was the color of the eyes that shook Birtles. In that creamy coffee face, they were a pale, transparent blue. Birtles could have believed they were contact lenses worn for some spectacular stage effect. The man clasped hands with Lucy and they went out into the gathering darkness.

His heart pounding, Birtles tossed back his drink and hurried after them. They were walking not far ahead, the Feather girl in flat shoes, her hips rolling provocatively, her loose-limbed companion padding beside her like some jungle animal. He stopped an approaching stranger, an American-looking youth, and said something. The young man produced a lighter and put a flame to the Eurasian's cigarette. Birtles noticed the American's face as he continued on and thought he looked dazed, as if he had been spoken to by a movie star. It must have been those eyes.

The couple went into a pub on the corner. Birtles gave them a minute to settle themselves, then followed them in. They were still at the bar. He worked his way through at the far end and ordered a pint. By the time it had been pulled and paid for, they were sitting on an upholstered bench, part of an island arrangement in the middle of the room.

Birtles was able to find a place to sit where his back was to them. He could make out only part of what was being said. The Eurasian had a quiet voice; his remarks to Lucy Feather came across as those of a patient father handling a difficult child. "It can be done," he said at one point. "Anything can be done." And later: "Isn't it enough just to go and let them wonder?"

Lucy's voice rose after a few minutes. "No, I can't. I was riding her a couple of days ago. You'll have to."

He felt his stomach tighten. A few days ago she was in his daughter's room, he had heard the hectoring voices through the wall. Was that what Lucy was referring to—had she been riding Barbie, nagging her about going to India? If so, what was it her companion would have to do?

Birtles stood and carried his glass on a wide circle so that he approached them from the bar. He managed to look surprised when his eyes met Lucy's, and before anything was said he slipped onto the bench beside her.

"Hello, Lucy. You don't recognize me. I'm Norman Birtle's, Barbie's father."

"Yes, of course." She was nervous. Her big, moist lips grimaced over perfect teeth. She tossed her head and her bound-up hair shook like a horse's mane. "This is my friend, Ezra Monty."

Monty gave Birtles a warm handshake. The blue crystal eyes met his and Birtles felt penetrated. He felt studied and stripped down and emptied out, but the surprising part of it was he didn't mind. A lot of casual conversation was going on and he couldn't have remembered a word of it.

"Well," Lucy was saying as he began to emerge from his stupor, "funny to run into you here. Quite a coincidence."

"I used to live around here," Birtles improvised. "I come back sometimes to see the old neighbourhood." They knew he was lying. There was an attentiveness around the table and Birtles imagined heads lifting in the jungle, nostrils sniffing the air.

"I'm worried about Barbie," he said to Lucy. "She left home the other night. I woke up in the morning and she was gone. With all her stuff."

"I understood she was leaving for Canada."

"Not till next week. And she'd never go without saying goodbye."

"Maybe she changed her mind. Maybe she just decided to go."

"Silently?" Birtles demanded. "In the dead of night?" He implied it was the sort of thing Lucy Feather might do to her parents, but not his daughter.

Monty leaned across Lucy and touched Birtles on the arm. "I understand your concern," he said. "I have many contacts in all sorts of places, I travel a good deal. Barbara Birtles—Lucy will give me a description. I'll put out the word. Don't worry, sir. We'll find your daughter."

It was an incredible sensation—Birtles felt as if a heavy load had been lifted from him. Ezra Monty was in charge and everything was going to be all right.

"And now"—Monty glanced at a sliver of gold in his wrist—"we have something we must attend to. Lucy?"

They were on their way out the door when the spell wore off and Birtles realized he mustn't lose them. More than ever, he sensed there was a link here with Barbara. He tried to drink some beer, almost choked on it, got up, and hurried out onto the dark street.

The couple were climbing into a car a short distance up Inverness Avenue. Birtles lurked in the pub entrance and watched them drive away with Lucy at the wheel. When they turned onto Bayswater Road and headed west, he began looking for a taxi. A car horn tooted, attracted his attention. It was Anitra in the Mini, cruising slowly toward him.

He climbed in beside her and slammed the door. "Bless your heart, I told you to go home."

"I thought you might need help."

"Turn right." She turned, causing a double-decker bus to brake and sound its horn. "There's a black Volvo ahead, can you see it?"

"In this traffic?"

"It's Lucy Feather and her boy friend. I talked to them in the pub. I have a feeling they're hiding something."

After driving as far as Notting Hill, Anitra said, "They could have gone anywhere. They might be on the way to the airport."

"I didn't see any luggage. They may be going to her place. Stop here." Birtles ran to a call box and checked the telephone directory. He found a Feather listed on Southside Common in Wimbledon. Back in the car, he gave Anitra the address and she took off. "Do me a favor," he said. "Keep me alive for a while longer."

Anitra's ability to cover the ground brought them to the Feather residence in record time. It was a three-storey gabled house that bespoke generations of money, probably starting with dividends from the East India Company. There was no black Volvo in sight.

"It was Heathrow like I said," Anitra predicted.

"Once around the Green," Birtles told her.

She took it easy and when they turned back onto Southside the Volvo was there. Anitra pulled over, engine off, lights out. Lucy got out of the car ahead and Ezra Monty followed, both easing the doors shut.

"Why are they acting like that? Isn't it her house?"

"It could be anything," Birtles said. Their movements as they left the car and crept down a laneway beside the house filled him with fear. They were like a military patrol out to silence an enemy position. During the drive he had told Anitra about the conversation in the pub. Now he said: "They might even have Barbie locked up here."

"Kidnapping? Is that possible? How would they have got her out of your place at night without your hearing them?"

Several minutes went by. Through the open window, Birtles could smell the delicious freshness from the Common, all those trees breathing in the night. Now there was movement at the entrance to the lane. Lucy ran out, turned and beckoned—she seemed impatient, in a state of high excitement. Monty followed and stood in front of the girl, put his hands on her shoulders, and shook her gently.

Her head fell back, and in the streetlight Birtles saw her eyes closed, her mouth open. If she had just inhaled some intoxicating substance, this would have been her reaction.

Monty fed her into the car and closed the door. He ran around and got in at the driver's side, switched on, and drove away. Birtles touched Anitra's shoulder and she began to drive ahead slowly. As they passed the laneway, he noticed something on the pavement. "Stop!" he told her and when she did he jumped out. By the time she parked and joined him, he was examining a dark wet smear on the concrete. He touched it and lifted his stained finger. "Blood," he said.

"Oh, God, get the police."

"I have to know. Have you got a flashlight in the car?" She ran away and brought it to him. He aimed its dim light at the ground and walked down the lane. Anitra kept close enough to touch a hand to his back every now and then.

They came to an out-building. The main house was a dark mass to the right. He saw grass, a concrete birdbath, rose bushes. The door was open in the shed beside him. As Birtles moved into the doorway, he smelled the pungent odor of a stable. He flashed the light over the board partitions of a stall, a leather harness on a hook, brass fittings, a saddle—then, on the stone floor, the body of a horse lying on its side. The animal was not quite dead—a leg kicked convulsively.

"Stay back." Birtles moved in closer, felt beneath his feet the pool of blood that Monty had tracked to the street, saw the gaping opening where the broad chestnut neck had been cut through. "Insane," he whispered. They're both insane..."

When they were driving again, he told Anitra to take him back to the hotel. She wanted to get the police but he said he was only concerned about his daughter and if they wasted one minute they might lose Feather and Monty. "I think they came out here to do this and now they'll be on their way."

"That must have been her own horse. Why would she kill it?"

"I don't know. In the pub she said, 'I was riding her a couple of days ago.' I thought she meant arguing with Barbie." Birtles nursed his fear as Anitra gunned down quiet roads.

When they arrived at the Candide, they found the Volvo parked outside. Anitra pulled in and idled. "The police?" she said plaintively. "Can we have the police now, please?"

"O.K. I'll get out and watch. You drive to the police station—there must be one near here. If you see a cop on the street, stop and tell him."

Birtles got out and positioned himself where he could watch the hotel entrance. The Mini wheeled down the street and turned the corner. Almost immediately, the glass door was pushed open by Monty carrying a couple of expensive-looking suitcases. Lucy Feather followed with a zippered flight bag. Monty loaded the luggage expertly, closed the trunk, and went to join Lucy in the front seat.

Birtles had to make up his mind. He ran forward, opened the back door, and slid inside just as the car pulled away.

Lucy glanced at him in the rearview mirror as she moved into traffic. "You again! What gives?"

"That's what I intend to find out. Why did you kill your horse?"

Her voice hardened. "Take care of him."

Monty turned and gave Birtles a look of admiration. "Were you out there tonight?"

"I'm looking for my daughter. I'm convinced you two know where she is."

"Why do you think that?"

"Because I found a Candide Hotel envelope in her room with some pot in it. And when I came down here I ran into you and Lucy. Lucy visited Barbara a few days ago—I heard them arguing in her room."

"He's quite a detective, Lucy. He's a determined man. I like that."

"All right," Lucy said. "I gave Barbara some stuff when I went to pick up the book. We argued because I wanted her to come with us but she wouldn't."

"End of story," Monty said. "We know nothing about your daughter, Mr. Birtles."

"I think you do. Anyway, we're going to have it out. My girl friend went to get the police."

Lucy gave him a contemptuous glance. "That's pathetic. Do you know who this is? I told you Ezra Monty—his real name is Eric Merlot. You know the book I got from Barbara? It's about him."

Birtles had read the book, had glanced at a couple of badly reproduced photos in the centerfold. This could be the man.

"He's killed eleven people already. You mean nothing to him. He'll blow you away as soon as look at you. Where shall we go, Eric? Out in the country?"

Merlot laughed and patted her shoulder. "She's my greatest admirer. When she heard there was a book about me, she had to get a copy right away." He became serious. "Nobody's killed anybody here and nobody's going to. This is England, not India. I said I like you, Mr. Birtles. Barbara's a lucky girl to have a father who cares about her as much as you do— I can tell you that from experience. And I can see the same qualities in you that I like in her."

"You've seen her then."

"Of course I have. I was keeping quiet because she asked me to. She's agreed to come east and work for me. I provide a service for young people traveling out there and Barbara would be ideal."

Birtles looked at the handsome face watching him across the upholstered seat. Those pale eyes caught what little light there was— all he could see was intelligent, honest, friendly eyes. "She never said anything to me."

"She wouldn't. She cares about your feelings. I'm offering her glamour, excitement, her own apartment in one of the nicer hotels in Singapore. That beats a cubbyhole bedroom with Daddy listening through the kitchen wall."

Nobody spoke for a few seconds. Then Birtles said: "You've been in my house, Mr. Merlot. When was that?"

"Eric, you're going to have to kill him. This is getting worse."

"Just drive the car. Mr. Birtles is an intelligent man. Sir, I'll admit I was there. We came in the other night using Barbara's key. She sent us to get her backpack. She'd decided to come with me. O.K.? I've told you the truth."

"And her traveller's checks. You got those too?"

"Of course. She said not to forget her traveller's checks."

"But one thing still doesn't fit. Even if Barbara had decided to go with you she would have told me. But she hasn't, and that means something's wrong."

"Eric?" Lucy said in a voice that combined a supplication and a warning.

"And if she's going with you to Singapore, how come you two are driving away without her?"

Merlot laughed. The laugh announced that Birtles was the most entertaining company he'd encountered in a long time. "I'm going to have to give you the rest of it. Barbara wanted your feelings spared—that's why you haven't heard from her. The fact is, she and I met through Lucy and there was this physical thing between us. Can you understand that? She moved in at the hotel and all she cared about was—well, two things. She also loved what I gave her to smoke. She's been stoned out of her mind for the past three days."

Birtles waited. Yes, he could believe any woman might become infatuated with Eric Merlot. He hated the idea of Barbie falling into that existence. But right now all he wanted was to find her and see that she was all right.

"I decided," Merlot continued, "that the best thing for me to do was disappear. Since she's so young. So I left her in the room at the Candide—I paid for another couple of days in advance. When she wakes up and sorts herself out, she'll come home. And, Mr. Birtles, please don't tell her where I've gone."

The car slowed down and halted at a traffic light. "I've been told so many things," Birtles said. "First, you were taking her to Singapore. Now you've left her and she doesn't know you've gone. It could all be lies."

"Shut up," Lucy snapped. "Just shut your mouth and get out of the car." She pulled on the hand brake, leaving herself free to sprawl back over the seat and open the back door. "Just get out and go away. And consider yourself lucky."

Birtles got out. He slammed the back door and opened the front door beside Merlot. He put an arm lock on the younger man's head and dragged him from the car. "You're going, too," he said. "I want you with me until I find my daughter."

The light changed. They were in one of the middle lanes and Birtles had to dodge cars as traffic began to move. Lucy had no choice but to drive on. When they reached the sidewalk, Merlot laughed in a high shrill voice. "Fabulous!" he screamed. "You incredible sonofabitch, that's the sort of thing I'd do!"

He was still laughing when they reached an Underground station. As they went down the steps, Merlot's arm firmly held by Birtles, the Eurasian said: "That's how I got away from the police in Rajasthan. Impulse. A window was open, so I climbed through and ran across a yard and out the gate. You keep your eyes open and you take quick, decisive action."

They missed a Central Line train heading east and had to wait on a deserted platform. Merlot glanced at the hand locked onto his upper arm. "Getting tired?" he asked. "I know how hard it is to hold somebody who doesn't want to be held. That's why I use a lot of drugs. You should buy me a coffee and put a few capsules in it."

Birtles pushed Merlot onto a bench and knelt before him. He took his right foot in both hands and twisted sharply. "Oh, Christ, no—" Merlot groaned. The bone snapped and Birtles released the foot.

"Now you won't run," he said. "Not on a broken ankle."

Merlot threw his head back so hard it hit the tiled wall. His eyes were glazed. "Sadistic bastard, you didn't have to do that."

"I think I did. Anyway, you killed that horse, don't talk to me about sadism."

Merlot struggled to get a handkerchief from his pocket. He wiped his eyes and blew his nose. "Want to know why we killed the horse? It was Lucy's idea. She's worse than both of us put together."

A train was approaching. Birtles drew Merlot up and supported him on the lame side. They boarded the train and the doors closed. They sat on a double seat.

"The horse," Merlot said. "I needed money and Lucy got it for me by selling some of her parents' things. Her father threatened to sell her horse to recoup the money. That was what made up her mind to come away with me. Before we left, she decided to kill the horse so they couldn't sell it."

"I think you two deserve each other," Birtles said grimly. "But God help the world if you should spawn."

Merlot laughed. "You think I'd marry or have children? Put more life into this rotten world? Have no fear."

When the train arrived at Queensway Station, Merlot's eyes were closed. As Birtles helped him onto the escalator, he asked: "How's the ankle?"

Merlot seemed still to be thinking of the absurdity of his marrying Lucy Feather. "She's just a contact for me in London—a source of money while I hide. A gang of English kids in Katmandu gave me her name. When I broke jail the last time, it gave me a place to come and stay."

The three-block walk to the hotel took time. Merlot gritted his teeth and limped on. His weight was light but his slender, supple frame reminded Birtles of the aluminum tent poles he used to erect on camping trips. They were practically unbreakable.

Approaching the Candide, he kept a lookout for a police presence. There was no sign of vehicles or uniformed men. Of course, Merlot had been gone for some time—Anitra would have returned with the police to be told their man had checked out. By now she and the police would be on the way to the airport.

Inside the hotel, on the stairs to his first-floor room, Merlot said: "Your daughter is O.K., I promise you that. When you're satisfied, will you let me go?"

"All I care about is Barbie," Birtles said. But did he mean that? The man on his shoulder was a murderer, escaped from police custody. He was a psychopath, capable of killing a horse with a knife. How could he be let free? He was smug and confident, holding in contempt the laws and the society that Birtles had supported all his life. "I don't care about you," he added.

"Then we understand each other," Merlot said in a quiet voice with just a trace of an edge.

Merlot had kept his key. As he unlocked the door of his room he glanced at Birtles and read the inquiry in his eyes. "There was no way Lucy was getting on that plane. I was going to give her the key and send her back to take care of Barbara. O.K.?"

They went inside where Merlot snapped on a light and closed the door. It turned out to be a small suite. He indicated a closed door. "She's in the bedroom."

"You, too," Birtles said, pulling Merlot with him.

Merlot opened the door and Birtles went into the bedroom. He saw a familiar shape in the bed, recognized the curly head on the pillow even in near darkness. He left the limping man and hurried to the bed. As he bent over her, Merlot turned on a lamp. The light fell on Barbie's face, undamaged but passive as a sculpture.

"Barbie? Love?" Birtles touched her cheek. There was warmth. "Are you all right?"

Her eyelids flickered, raised—she saw him and immediately there were tears. "Oh, it's you," she slurred. "Daddy, I was hoping you'd come—"

"I'm here now. You'll be O.K."

"They gave me drugs. They wanted my money. I couldn't phone, I couldn't move or do anything."

"I'll get a doctor for you. We'll have you home in no time."

"Daddy, I'm not going away. I'm going to stay with you—"

"Shhhh." She had reverted to the school girl who used to feign illness so she could stay home in bed where he would bring her lunch on a tray and the deck of cards for a game of rummy. "We'll talk about it when you're better."

He heard the bedroom door close, heard the snap of a key in the lock. He got up and ran to the door. "Merlot, don't be crazy!"

"She's O.K., right? That's my side of the bargain. I don't trust you, Mr. Birtles—I'm off."

"You'll get nowhere on that ankle."

"Pain is all in the mind. I've turned off worse than this when I had to."

Birtles hit the door with his fist. It was old-fashioned, a solid, heavy panel. "Merlot!"

"I've been in three jails and got out every time. You never had a hope of holding me." His voice drew away. "Goodbye, Mr. Birtles, you'll never see me again. Too bad— I like you." The outer door closed.

Birtles went back to the bed. "Barbie, I'm going to make some noise. I have to break the door. Don't worry, I'll be back soon."

She gave him the wise, mature smile—his mother encouraging him to do his best. He went back to the door and balanced himself. It took five lunges to put his boot through the panel. A minute later, he was outside and running for the stairs.

The lobby was deserted, nobody on duty at the desk. Merlot was crafty enough to be hiding somewhere inside, but Birtles decided to have a quick look on the street. Self-hypnosis or whatever, he couldn't be covering the ground very quickly.

Outside, he saw a crowd gathering at the corner of Bayswater Road. He stared and could hardly believe his eyes when he made out what looked to be the familiar blue Mini. Running in that direction, he picked out Anitra Colahan's peach coiffure glistening under the street lamp in the midst of the crowd.

He reached her and when she saw him she took his arm for support. "Oh, God, he ran right in front of the car! You weren't here when I got back with the police. I was cruising the neighborhood looking for you. I turned the corner and he was running across—not running, limping."

"It's O.K." Birtles looked down, saw the pale-blue eyes staring. Somebody would have to close them for him now. "That's Merlot, the man who was holding Barbara. They drugged her to rob her. He's killed a lot of people."

Anitra turned away. A police car was pulling up. "Here they come," she said grimly. "Three tries to get my license and now I'm going to lose it."

Birtles looked from her to the dead man and back at her angry face. All right, so there were signs all around that it was indeed the selfish, imperfect world Merlot believed it to be. Not so long ago it was a jungle and people were eating each other.

"When you've given the cops your statement," he said, "come back to the hotel. I'll be with Barbie, waiting for the doctor. When she's taken care of, you can drive me home."

As he walked away, Birtles realized he'd just told Anitra that he loved her.

Fear is a Killer

Originally published in *Ellery Queen Mystery Magazine*, December 1986.

WITH HIS HEART POUNDING, WALTER WINGBEAT SAT AT the boardroom table half listening to what Clay Fetterson was telling the client. "Nor do we usually formulate an advertising plan before the product is developed and tested. But in this case, at your request—"

As the head of R&B Advertising continued his preamble, Wingbeat glanced from face to face around the mahogany oval. The client, Norman Imrie, president of Metro Distillers, was looking noble. Sensing Wingbeat's attention, Imrie returned an encouraging smile. Tough, but fair and decent—that was Mr. Imrie.

"So—we have prepared, among other exhibits," Fetterson continued, "a media plan. But before I ask our media manager to take us through it, may I voice anxiety over the name of the new product. A liqueur distilled in America is a great idea. Using the flowers of an indigenous desert plant gives us something to talk about in the advertising. But for a drink, the name Yucca..."

Wingbeat was turning his pages. He remembered what it was to breathe deeply but the technique had escaped him for the moment. The imaginary iron strapping around his chest was at maximum clamp. Pinprick bubbles of light fizzed around the periphery of his vision.

A hand touched his. A voice murmured, "Are you all right?" It was Penelope Good, the girl from England. He had hired her as his assistant three months ago. The department was in need of people but Wingbeat was afraid to hire. What if he chose the wrong person? In Miss Good, it looked as if he had brought in somebody very good indeed. And now he was a afraid of that.

He managed a smile, glazed eyes and sick lips that would have stampeded nurses in an intensive-care unit. "Butterflies," he whispered, fluttering a flat hand. "Okay once I start."

She made a kissing face at him. It was way out of line, he hadn't even taken her to lunch yet. Her honey hair was much too smart for the money she earned. How did she manage? Her suit looked expensive. Her blue eyes were calm. Penelope Good fitted in around the executive table like the maroon-leather armchairs themselves.

"Not to worry," she mouthed silently, "I'm with you."

Apprehension about the new brand-name had been expressed to Norman Imrie before. "Be assured, gentlemen and lady," he said, "the name Yucca has been thoroughly tested. I went around my office and spoke to twenty people. Told them my wife had come up with a concept and a name for a new liqueur. Yucca. What did they think? Not one negative reaction. One hundred percent in favor."

Clay Fetterson's grin became brighter than a thousand suns. Wingbeat had to avert his eyes as the boss said, "Can't argue with research as conclusive as that. On we go. Let's take a look at the media plan. Everybody got a copy? Fine. Wally, will you lead us through this?"

"Uh, sure, Clay." Wingbeat was alone, terrified. "These are rough figures, guesstimates, because I was told I wouldn't see budget until after the taste-testing, which I understand is not happening until—"

"Could you just take us through it, Wally?"

"Sure, Clay. Uh, page one is a summary of the major markets, with some additional weighting in—" The iron bands tightened. Wingbeat's breath was reduced to a flutter. "Oh, wow," he said, as panic took over.

"Everything okay, Wally?"

Elbows on the table, Wingbeat put a flat hand on either side of his face, shutting out witnesses to his humiliation. To die like this in public—Trouble breathing. Just a minute."

"Is there pain?" The observers were riveted. They were not callous people but if the media manager went in mid-presentation—would that be a story to dominate drinks this evening.

"Not a lot of pain," Wingbeat said. He was coming out of it. It was stress, tension. "Have to get my breath."

"Should the man try to continue?" Norman Imrie asked. He was less entertained than the others. "Give him a rest."

"Exactly right," Fetterson said. "Can you take over, Miss Good? Wally, slide over to the couch. Put your feet up."

As Wingbeat left the table, Penelope Good unbuttoned her jacket to reveal a nicely rounded white silk blouse. Placing a fist on her hip authoritatively, she said in a voice worthy of the Royal Shakespeare Company, "The summary requires less than a glance at this time. May I direct your attention to the following pages, where, market by market, we see the media breakdown. Forgive the word 'breakdown', Walter," she said and everybody laughed, including Wingbeat.

As was his habit, Wingbeat worked a couple of extra hours after closing to give the Friday-evening traffic a chance to clear. By the time he drove home and parked his car in the driveway that separated his cedar-and-stone bungalow from the brick-and-stucco cottage next door, his wife and son had finished their supper. Corliss was in a deckchair on the back lawn under one of the stately poplars, holding a depleted glass of gin and tonic in her hand. A glow and babble from the television room showed where young Philip was hiding.

"Cold plate in the fridge," Corliss said as she accepted her evening kiss. There was a book opened face-down on her lap, something heavy from the non-fiction bestsellers list. Corliss Wingbeat was never seen without a book, but she seldom read anything clear through. Her last conquest dated back several years—Jonathon Livingston Seagull.

Wingbeat ate his salad standing up in the kitchen. Taking food out-of-doors in view of the neighbors gave him a queasy feeling. After rinsing and stacking his plate, he wandered through to change this clothes. On the way past the TV room, he looked in on Philip, who smiled tenderly at him as he reduced the sound.

"Evening, Pip," Walter said to his eleven-year-old. "Shouldn't you be outside enjoying the glorious fresh air?"

"Same air in here, Father." The boy indicated the open window.

"You have a point." Wingbeat lingered.

"Is everything all right?" Pip was watching his father's face.

"Just fine! It's the weekend!" The distressed adman clapped his hands and executed a buck-and-wing. The step was not badly done. A generation ago, he had sparkled as one of the policemen in a high school production of The Pirates of Penzance.

"You look sad, Father."

"The mature face in repose, my son. Nothing to be alarmed about. How's this?" Wingbeat hooked an index finger in either side of his mouth and dragged his lips upwards into a manic smile. At the same time he let his eyes go crossed. Philip fell over, laughing and rolling on the carpet and Wingbeat walked away feeling good for the first time in days.

When he appeared on the back lawn ten minutes later, dressed in slacks and T-shirt and his recently whited tennis shoes, the sun was setting. Its last rays picked out the awkwardly sporty figure and made him glow. The raucous voice of Wingbeat's neighbor, Larry Boxer, filled the silence.

"Hey, Wally," he bellowed, "dim your shoes!"

As Wingbeat dragged a chair across the grass and sat close to his wife, she muttered, "Why don't you tell that oaf to shut his big mouth?"

"He's only kidding."

"You let people push you around, Walter. It isn't good for you. What are you afraid of?"

"I'm not afraid."

"You are." Corliss raised her voice just enough. "You reek fear."

"I've never seen the sense in contention. Why argue with people? Cooperation is more productive." He had not played his trump card in months. Tonight it seemed risky but he threw it down anyway. "It works for me. I'm the head of media in one of Canada's leading ad agencies." Secretly, Wingbeat knew why they kept him in the job. Because he worked all the hours God sends, not employing extra staff, keeping the department budget low. He would never say this to his wife. He was afraid to.

Corliss finished her third drink. She was feeling comfortably aggressive. "How is the smarmy limey?" she asked.

He knew she was referring to Penelope Good. There had been bad blood between the two women since an office party a couple of months ago at which the English newcomer mistook Corliss Wingbeat for catering staff, handing her an empty glass. "Who?"

"You know who. Penelope Put-down. I'd keep an eye on her. She wants your job. And God help her if she takes it." Corliss modified her threat. "God help you."

"We can help each other," Penelope said, glancing at Clay Fetterson for confirmation. The hotel dining room was medium busy for two o'clock. It was unusual for Walter Wingbeat to be lunching in such surroundings at such an hour. His normal lunch was tuna salad on whole wheat taken at his desk along with yet another mug of company coffee.

"My idea exactly," the managing director said. "You obviously need relief, Wally. We don't want a repetition of the seizure episode last week. Bad impression in front of the client. I know it's illogical but it could make him think R&B Advertising is not healthy."

"It hasn't happened before," Wingbeat said. "Shouldn't happen again." Fear flooded his belly.

"We're seeing to that," the boss said. "Penny will take on the executive responsibilities. She will confront ferocious clients in their dens. Meanwhile, the wealth of Wingbeat experience will still be ours to tap when and as we need it."

Penelope could only repeat what she had said before. "We can help each other." But her grin was tight and she swallowed without drinking or eating anything.

"And now," Fetterson said, "we'd better get back to the office. At four-thirty, we taste-test Metro Distillers' newest product, Yucca Liqueur."

"Yeeuch!" Penelope said, pretending to recoil as the managing director landed a playful punch on her arm.

*　*　*　*

Testing a client's product was almost like being let out of school. Opinions were so widely sought that every member of the agency staff, from Clay Fetterson himself on down to the lowliest filing clerk, was welcomed into the boardroom to join the party and put forward an opinion. This product being made with alcohol, the session was scheduled for late in the working day. By five o'clock closing time the room looked and sounded something like happy hour at a neighborhood bar.

Several bottles of Yucca stood open on the mahogany table, protected now with a linen cover. Almost everyone punctuated the first sip of the liqueur with the spontaneous reaction—"Yeeuch!"

"That name has got to go," a copywriter on the account would say and the crowd would laugh.

But the sober truth was, the stuff did taste vile. Nobody wanted a second glass of it—except for Penelope Good. The English import swilled the liqueur down and became merrier by the minute. "Jolly nice," she commented. "Not finishing your sample, love? Waste not, want not, I'll just tip your glass into mine."

Wingbeat was among those who abominated the mickey-mouse booze. But, a solid agency man, he appreciated the fact that Yucca was the brainchild of the client's wife and he knew they would have to sell it.

Wife. Watching Penelope getting high, he brooded. Here was his replacement as head of the department. Soon it would be made public and Corliss would have to know. Staff might accept the change and forget about it but his wife would not take it easily.

"Cheer up, Wally," Fetterson said, his overfed face florid with good-fellowship. "It may never happen."

"It already has."

"You hate presenting to clients. You'll be happier out of the rat-race."

"There are others involved."

Fetterson, a married man, knew what his former media chief was getting at. "Explain to Corliss. Tell her the job was killing you."

Wingbeat left the session. He fled to the safety of his desk, lost himself in pages of figures which demanded nothing of him except that he arrange them in columns that added up. Never mind the job killing him. Robbed of her prestige as wife of a manager, deprived of the extra money that went with the responsibility, Corliss would make his life not worth living.

The idea entered Wingbeat's troubled mind without preamble. Kill or be killed. It was preposterous, but perhaps it was the only way. Not Corliss—he would never murder his wife. But if he could find some safe way to terminate Penelope Good's stay on the planet, his problem would disappear.

Wingbeat was so shaken by the possibility that he left the office earlier than usual and drove home in rush-hour traffic. His street looked different at a quarter to six, with men getting out of cars and wives greeting them. Larry Boxer was opening his front door, jacket off, shirt sleeves rolled, bulging briefcase hinting at problems the jovial salesman faced like anybody else.

"What happened, Wally?" he called. "Fired at last?"

"Not yet, Larry." Wingbeat was so harassed, he let fly an answering salvo. "But when they drop me, I'm coming over to live off you."

Inside the house, he took his wife and son by surprise. They were playing dominos at the kitchen table. Corliss had her first gin and tonic beside her. Philip was getting through milk and cookies.

"Good Lord," Corliss said, as if a game-show host had climbed out of the television set.. "What are you doing here?"

"I live here. Hello, dear." He kissed her and ruffled the cornsilk hair on his son's giant head. "Evening, Pip." As he moved off to change his clothes, he said, "Think I'll do a little gardening. Not hungry yet."

"Have you been drinking?"

"Taste-testing. Metro's new liqueur."

"Is it as bad as it smells?"

Ten minutes later, wearing an R&B sweatshirt and the trousers he was proud of because of their grass-stained knees, Wingbeat hurried down to the gardening shed and brought out clippers, rake, work-gloves, and a plastic bag for rubbish. The tin of weed-killer was almost full. He took it to the light and began reading the copy on the label. It certainly carried enough warnings about the danger of swallowing the stuff.

"Father?" Philip was watching him.

"Hello again, Pip." He felt uncomfortable, caught in the act. "Nothing on the box just now? Aren't they rerunning Dr. Who?"

"Can I help you? I want to help."

"Take the clippers and go up to the rock garden. Trim the grass between the rocks."

"What are you going to be doing?"

"Finishing reading this." Empathy between father and son was intense. Wingbeat had to turn away as his eyes filled up. "Get on with it, son," he said. "Dad needs to be alone."

Early next morning, briefcase in hand, Wingbeat left the breakfast table and walked not to his car but across the back lawn to the gardening shed. Inside, he opened the briefcase, took up the tin of weed-killer, fitted it carefully inside between files, then closed the case.

"What gives?" Corliss called from the doorway as he came back and let himself into the car. Pip's calm face watched from the kitchen window.

"Left my watch on the shelf last night," he said, raising his wrist as an exhibit. It was no lie. Anticipating such a question, he had taken off his watch and left it in the shed before going after dandelions last night with a rusty knife.

Penelope Good paid him a short visit at half past nine, perching on his spare chair, crossing her shiny legs and swallowing coffee from a mug with "Carnaby Street" silk-screened on it. Then, "Must run, love," she said. Penny called everybody love, or ducks. "The idiot in the corner office wants to pick my brains about a new-business presentation."

Her irreverence about Fetterson only made Wingbeat wonder how she talked about him in front of others. "All right, love," he said. "Did you enjoy the Yucca tasting?"

"Fabulous. I can't understand why the others were putting it down."

Wingbeat had smuggled a full bottle out of the boardroom. He opened his bottom drawer and lifted the jug into view. "Play your cards right—" he hinted.

"Yummy-yum," the girl said, rounding her eyes.

"You never know your luck in a big city," he told her. "This could be the day!"

When she was gone, he closed his door. He found a sheet of clean paper and folded it crisply. He twisted open the cap on the bottle and removed it. He took the tin of weed-killer from his briefcase and poured a quantity of the white powder into the V of the folded paper. Then he funneled the poison carefully into the bottle, tapping the paper to expedite the flow. Last of all, he capped the bottle, turning it a few times to disperse the powder. The bottle stored away, he opened the door, went back to his chair, and lost himself in a forest of numbers.

At four-thirty, Wingbeat wrapped the bottle in a brown-paper bag left over from one of his frugal lunches. Then he got into his jacket, took hold of his briefcase in one hand and the bag in the other, and walked down the hall to Penelope's office. She was on the telephone, shoes tumbled on the carpet, stocking-feet propped on her desk. As she spoke and listened, she read her visitor in the doorway, his face, his briefcase, the rounded paper bag. The silky toes crimped and flexed.

"Is this an imposition?" Wingbeat asked when, at last, she terminated her call. "I know it isn't closing time yet, but this bottle needs drinking. And you do enjoy the stuff. And I used to be manager of this department and you soon will be, so between the two of us we ought to be free to—"

"Say no more, say no more." The girl got up and slipped her feet into the alligator high-heels. She put on a Charles Boyer voice... "Come wiz me to ze Casbah. I have cheese to go wiz de booze!"

The receptionist performed not a double, but a triple-take as she saw the unlikely couple vanish into an elevator. "Strategy conference," Penelope called as the door slid shut.

Home from school, Philip Wingbeat raised suspicion in his mother's mind by not raiding the refrigerator directly. "Are you all right?" she asked him.

"Worried."

"What about? Damn it, you've been sleeping in class again, I'm going to have to pay yet another boring visit to placate the principal."

"Worried about Father. He seems depressed."

"He enjoys it. If it wasn't for me pushing him, he'd be shining shoes at Central Station."

Philip could not bring himself to mention the weed-killer. His silence on the subject had something to do with preserving his father's dignity. But he was determined to sound a warning. After that, he would have done everything in his power.

"Mother, it isn't like other times. I think he may try something. Father needs help."

Corliss Wingbeat heard something in her son's voice. An alarm rang inside her head. Walter had come home on time from work the other night. That was definitely odd. The boy's rapport with his father was close. "You may be right," she said. Leaving her chair, she went and found her purse, throwing in wallet and car keys. It was one thing to tease Walter in a casual way, but she wanted him secure for quite a few years yet. "I'll collect your father at the office. We'll have supper out. I'll talk to him. Feed yourself from the fridge, darling."

Corliss drove in the opposite direction to the main flow of traffic, arriving at the R&B offices just as the receptionist was putting things away. "I'm sorry, you've missed him, Mrs. Wingbeat," the girl said. She could hardly believe her luck. Wingbeat's wife never came to get him. And tonight of all nights!

"I can't have missed him. It's barely five o'clock."

"He left early." The smile came easily. "Along with Penny Good. They said they were going for a strategy conference."

By a heroic effort, Corliss managed to conceal most of her fury from this twerpy girl. "Have you any idea where they're holding their conference?"

"Penny's apartment isn't far from here." The receptionist checked a list in a rare display of efficiency. She recited the address, adding, "It's the old converted building around the corner."

* * * *

Walter Wingbeat was surprised at the smart interior of the apartment, situated as it was in such a grotty old structure. He said so as
he cracked the cap on the bottle of Yucca, pretending he was breaking a seal.

"Thanks," Penelope said. "I badgered the landlord into plastering
the cracks and painting. The rest I did myself. But the exterior is not
to be believed. I shudder at the thought of a fire." She produced two
tumblers. "Sorry I don't have liqueur glasses."

"You'll buy a nice set of crystal," Walter confided, pouring a gen-
erous measure of the ruby liquid into one of the tumblers," out of
your first pay as department head. Listen, have you got any juice or
mineral water? I'm not as keen on this stuff as you are."

"Hurray, more for me!" She brought him a bottle of fizzy orange.
"You're awfully good about this job change," she said. "Some men
would be homicidal."

"Truth is, the stress was killing me. You've done me a favor, you
and Fetterson." He poured his orange, toasted her, drank as heartily
as she did. The important thing, the reason for his being here, would
be to get rid of the remains of the poisoned liqueur after she keeled
over. Then, to fake illness himself. When she was well and truly
deceased, he would come around and telephone for an ambulance.
Too late.

"Yeeuch!" the English girl said with delight. She poured the drink
down her throat and reached for the bottle. "I don't care if the public laughs at the name and hates the product. I shall drink all they
can produce."

Nearly an hour had passed and half the bottle of cactus liqueur
was in Penelope Good's stomach when the door buzzer sounded.
Wingbeat's terror had been mounting, drink by drink. He had put in
enough poison to fell a rhino. His former assistant was very merry
indeed, but she showed no signs even of a mild tummy upset, let
alone death by weed-killer. "I'm going to answer the door," Penny
slurred. "If I should return during my absence, please notify me."

Wingbeat had no place to go. The apartment was of the bed-sit-
ting room variety with kitchenette attached. His alternatives were to

hide in the bathroom or a closet or else stay put and face the visitor. When it turned out to be Corliss, with an expression on her face of curiosity mixed with repressed fury, Wingbeat panicked. He had never been so terrified in his life. His mind couldn't produce a logical assessment. All it could contribute was the idea, "Out, out, out!" His wife was blocking the doorway, flanked by Penelope Good, who was smirking from one shell-like ear to the other. The window! There was no other escape route.

Flinging aside a length of curtain, he hoisted the sash and stepped through onto the iron-barred platform of a fire escape. A paved parking lot lay three floors below.

"I wouldn't!" his hostess called.

As if to substantiate her warning, the rickety construction squealed, a couple of rusty bolts slipped out of crumbling concrete moorings, and the fire escape swung out and away from the wall. "Hey!" Walter yelled. Now he really had something to be afraid about.

Corliss and Penelope were framed in the open window. His wife did the usual—she demanded something from him that he could not deliver. "Get back in here!" she yelled.

The English girl was shrieking with delight. "You look so funny! I love it! Your wife showed up and you actually—This is fabulous!" And then, having spent a part of her life being pummeled and battered in an English private school, and on her holidays falling out of boats or off of mountains in Europe, the bold young woman said, "Hang on, love. I'm coming to get you."

Wingbeat watched her kick off her shoes. He stared in fascination as her nylon-clad toes took purchase on the window ledge. "Don't move," she said. She tried a step forward onto the platform. It was too far away from the wall. "Give me your hand. And hold on. We'll drag you back."

It was a moment of focus. Walter Wingbeat saw his manifold fears now combined in the person of this optimistic girl. She had taken over his job. He was afraid to pass the terrible news on to his wife. The future was unbearable. If only Penelope Good did not exist.

Her arm was extended, her hand inches away. The decision was made for him by a survivor inside, a Wingbeat of whose existence he was only dimly aware. He grasped her hand, took his tightest grip, then gave a sudden, ferocious pull. It was as if he was taking her to him and her face brightened mischievously, but only for a split second because there was no place for her to go but down. She swore, two blunt words he was surprised to discover in her vocabulary. A moment later, she was spread-eagled between cars on the pavement. The building superintendent, who had been watching the drama, ran to examine the body.

Corliss raised her eyes. They met his. The glance asked many questions as it seemed to supply some answers. No heroine, Corliss Wingbeat solved the risky problem simply. "Get in here," she snapped. And her husband obediently took a long stride forward onto the window ledge and allowed himself to be dragged inside.

The super's testimony backed up the story of the surviving couple. It was embarrassing for the Wingbeats, but there was no case against them. Fleeing husband, angry wife. Brave mistress accidentally falls to her death. Misadventure.

The Wingbeat case could not be dismissed so easily at the office, however. Norman Imrie was a bit of a prude. Such goings-on between employees of his ad agency were not acceptable. So the offending department head had to be retired early. But the liquor tycoon was nothing if not fair. The man ought not to be penalized financially. Imrie let it be known that Wingbeat should receive his full pension. And it was done.

For the first time in his life, Walter Wingbeat had nothing to be afraid of. His income was guaranteed, his pension linked to the inflation rate. He had nothing to do these days but work around the garden and spend some time handicapping the thoroughbreds at Blue Bonnets. A few days later, Corliss came to where he was sitting on a bench by the garden shed. She had a cup of coffee for him and a suspicious frown on her face. She sat down.

"Spill it, Walter. You were up to something. A philanderer you're not."

He decided to level with her. "She was about to take over my job. I wanted to get rid of her. I put weed-killer in a bottle of Yucca liqueur and gave it to her. The poison could never be tasted in that horrible stuff. The reason I went to her apartment was so that nobody else would drink some accidentally. But it had no effect, the powder must have lost its potency."

"Fortunately for you. You must have been crazy." She showed him affection over his foolish behavior. " Had she died like that, there would have been an autopsy. They'd have discovered the poison. You gave her the bottle, you'd have been hauled up in court."

Wingbeat shrugged. "I wasn't thinking straight. Anyway, it didn't happen."

Corliss Wingbeat's fond mood lasted for the rest of the day. She decided to make her husband a bowl of his favorite vanilla pudding. Nobody else liked it, he could have what was left of the nearly full box of pudding powder she had found inside the pedalbin a few days ago. She asked Pip if he'd thrown it out and he said no, but who else would have done it? Maybe he was afraid he'd be given the hated pudding for dessert one day.

The boy fled that confrontation wondering if he should have spread the weed-killer around the garden instead of substituting it for something harmless. But somebody would have noticed the powder on the ground and he might have been observed had he tried to dig it in. Trust his mother to inspect the trash. Never mind—as long as the stuff was thrown out, it didn't matter that she suspected him of putting it there. Thus Philip Wingbeat worried the matter round and round. He had noticed that as he got older, he was more frightened of things.

In the kitchen, Corliss got out the pudding powder and the milk and a bowl and a whisk and gave herself a few minutes' exercise whipping up the mixture. When it was set, she brought it into the garden, where Walter was resting on the lounge swing with a pen and a pad and the daily racing form. "Here," she said, handing him the bowl and a spoon. "Just to let you know how I feel about you."

"Hey!" Wingbeat said. He scooped up a spoonful and swallowed it. It tasted odd—milky and bitter—but he was afraid to say anything that might destroy Corliss's friendly mood. So, with appropriate noises, he wolfed down the entire nasty mess while his wife watched and wondered how much longer she could survive, shackled to this irritating man.

The Last Act was Deadly

Originally published in *Alfred Hitchcock Mystery Magazine*, June 1978.

THE ROOMING HOUSE STUCK AWAY ON A BACK STREET in Brighton had nothing going for it, not even a view of the sea. But it served meals all day, something rare for English eating places, and the front door had a homely appeal, so Eric Tennyson walked under the enamelled sign advertising "Bed and Breakfast," pushed open the lace-curtained door, and went inside.

He knew it was a good choice the minute he entered the vestibule. The cooking smells, the fringe of tattered carpet meeting a crust of worn linoleum, the thickly overpainted woodwork, and the patterned wallpaper populated with framed faded photographs all reminded him of the house he had grown up in back in Vermont. He chose a table in the empty dining room and sat down on a hard caneback chair. The table, covered with a flowered cloth, teetered under his elbows.

A tall grey woman in a black-and-white uniform under a thin cardigan came into the room and stood over him with tiny fists clenched against her chest. She looked at him fondly and Tennyson was ready to be asked if he had done his homework and to get his skates off the kitchen floor. He glanced at the menu and ordered cod and chips.

"Do you want that with bread and butter and a cup to tea? You get cod-and-chips-and-bread-and-butter-and-a-cup-of-tea, 85 pence."

"Lovely," Tennyson said. "I'll have that." He had been long enough in London to learn to say "lovely."

The food came and the crisp brown slabs of breaded fish were quite simply the most delicious he had ever tasted. He soaked on the vinegar and salt, took a bite from a triangle of buttered bread, slurped a swallow of strong tea, and began really to enjoy himself.

It was a perfect example of the rewards that can come from obeying an impulse. The idea of taking this day-trip to Brighton had only occurred to him at breakfast. The sky was clear, Capital Radio said no rain all day, and his writing schedule was up to date, so he was free to walk to Wimbledon Station, take a train to Clapham Junction, and transfer there to the Brighton express. One hour later he was at the seaside—in June, before the main press of tourists.

Tennyson could hardly stop congratulating himself. His main venture during the afternoon had been a walk along the cliffs to the village of Rottingdean, three miles away. Here he drank lager in a couple of pubs, wandered the tidy streets, and spent an hour in and around a church that dated back to the Saxons.

Then he bussed back to Brighton and roamed the Palace Pier, dropping pennies into the sweeper machines, hoping to cause a penny avalanche over one of the ledges, eating licorice allsorts from a bag in his pocket, lying in a deck chair with his face to the sun.

He even entered the little toy house of Eva Montenegro, the famous Romany clairvoyant, and paid £3 to have his fortune told. She sat opposite him, grainy-faced and clear-eyed, warning him not to put his hands where she had just spilled her tea. Then she nattered on with a stream of consciousness that could have been about him, reading his reactions he supposed, shaping her talk according to the way his shrugs or eyebrows guided her.

One thing she said surprised and pleased him. "You do some writing—you are a clerk?"

"Not a clerk. I do write."

"Ah. You will write a good story. A big story will be a big success."

Tennyson wandered on the seafront afterwards with eyes half closed, his mind floating on her prediction. The dramatic society in Wimbledon had agreed to perform his play in the fall. It was only an amateur group, to be sure, and there would be no money in it. But he didn't require money. What he craved was success and here was the gypsy telling him he would have it.

Empty plates were taken away, the woman brought him a dish of apple pie with hot custard, and the delightful supper went on.

Then everything crashed as Tennyson looked up through the doorway into the vestibule and saw Meredith Morgan. He wanted to hide beneath the table. Of all people—the one member of the Hartfield Dramatic Society who really put him off—and here she was, not ten feet away. Fortunately, she had not seen him yet.

And what was this? She set a large suitcase at her feet and, raising her voice, she called straight ahead into the body of the house, "Hello? Anybody is at home, yes?"

Tennyson stopped tasting what he was eating. The accent was pure German, strong and true. Could it be Meredith Morgan's continental double? No, it was herself—it had to be. He had seen her only last week at a cast reading.

An invisible landlord made terms for a single room and Tennyson could hear Meredith hissing her stagey German as she signed the book. Then she reappeared beyond the dining-room doorway to claim her suitcase and Tennyson turned his head hard away. When he looked again, she was gone and he heard footsteps on a stairway.

There was absolutely no doubt in his mind that this was the Morgan girl and here she was in Brighton pretending to be a German tourist. Tennyson was intrigued now that the immediate danger of having to spend time with her was past. Not that there was much chance of her trapping and boring him; she was surely less anxious to meet him than he was to meet her.

But what was she up to? Tennyson finished his pie, scraping the last of the yellow custard from the dish, and considered the possibilities. The most preposterous occurred to him first. She was some sort of a spy. But that made no sense at all. If she did some work for M15 or whoever, she might end up in Berlin playing the part of a German. But in Brighton?

Perhaps it was a romantic involvement. She had a boy friend who, for some reason, thought she was from Germany and she was here for a liaison, carrying on the charade. But Meredith with a boyfriend, secret of otherwise, was hard to swallow. She was the least-liked individual in the Hartfield, by both men and women, and she took no pains to make herself more appealing.

Then Tennyson thought of a far-fetched notion that might explain her behavior. Somewhere down the road the Society was going to do a play in which there was a female part demanding a German accent. Meredith wanted the role so she had come here to live for a few days as a German, getting dialect practice all day long. Possible but, on second thought, doubtful. She could do this in London—no need to come to Brighton.

Tennyson paid for his supper and went outside. He had gone a dozen paces down the cobbled lane when the impulse hit him and he returned, entering a pub opposite the rooming house, ordering a pint at the bar, and taking it to a table near the front window. He sat down and began watching the painted doorway. It had become very important for him to learn why Meredith Morgan was in Brighton, pretending to be Marlene Dietrich.

As he drank his beer, Tennyson remembered his early days in England, over a year ago. He had settled in Wimbledon simply because the name of the place meant something to him from years of following tennis. And it had lots of Underground and British Rail trains to and from London. Since his aim in life was to become a successful playwright, now that he was financially independent for a few years thanks to a state lottery win, it made sense for Tennyson to become involved with a theatrical group. The West End was beyond him at present, so it had to be an amateur society.

That was how he came to seek out the Hartfield. They were a friendly group and apparently happy to accept a good-looking, 28-year-old American, although his accent certainly did not blend with theirs onstage. Now, after playing small parts in three productions, Tennyson had made the breakthrough he was seeking; they were going to do his play, Call It Love, as their September production. It was a romantic comedy, set in Wimbledon, with a tennis background.

As a group, the Hartfield could only be called jovial. They kidded Tennyson about some of his pronunciations, praised his forceful acting style, and waved to him on the street. He was on a cheek-kissing basis with most of the girls. But not with Meredith Morgan. At first, he took the conversational initiative with her and attributed her monosyllabic replies to shyness but after a while he tired of it and stopped speaking to her—let her make the effort.

Onstage, at the close of one play, he found himself placed next to her in the curtain-call lineup. Automatically, as they bowed, he took the hand of the person on either side of him. Meredith's hand, cold and claw-like, tore itself free and he did not touch her again.

There was movement in the doorway across the street. Meredith emerged dressed in shades of blue—a tight T-shirt, short skirt, and plastic boots. This was nothing like what she wore back in Wimbledon and Tennyson felt a quickening of his heartbeat as he finished his beer and left the pub.

She turned left at the main road and wandered down the hill towards the seafront. It was becoming dark and strings of lights sparkled along the broad walk. Beyond, the English Channel, flat on this calm night, was fading to black. Tennyson was not surprised to see pedestrians, men and women, turning to look at the attractive girl in blue as they passed her.

This new style of hers puzzled Tennyson as much as anything, because at rehearsals Meredith was a mouse. His impression of her there, whenever he bothered to look, was of furtive brown eyes, unwashed short brown hair, hungry cheeks, and sloping posture, usually with an inch or two of unstitched hem at the bottom of her skirts.

Now she swaggered ahead of him, swinging a red plastic handbag, trailing her fingertips on building fronts—arrogant, provocative. Tennyson worked to control his breathing as he followed her into a pub called The Cutlass. He used his head and came in right after her, reasoning that given time she would be seated and possibly watching the door.

He was able to watch her order a gin and tonic and carry it to a table in an alcove. Tennyson brought his beer with him and sat on the other side of the upholstered parapet where he could see and hear the girl without being seen, unless she turned fully around.

The action was not long in starting. Meredith finished her drink quickly and set down the empty glass. A middle-aged man, heavy-set and grey-headed, took his own glass and reached for hers. "Same again, love?" he said. His accent was from somewhere up north.

"Thank you, you are very kind. It is gin and tonic."

He returned with the refills and hers looked like a double. "Cheers, love," he said, and after they drank he went on, "Well then, how do you like our country?"

"I am only here one day but it is very good. The people are so friendly."

"Famous for it," the man said. "And where's home?"

"I come from Hamburg. That is in Germany."

"I know where Hamburg is."

"Ah, you have been there?"

"Yes, but not to stay. I flew over in a Lancaster, long before you were born. All I saw was a lot of fires burning." He was well away on the beer and the effect of it could be heard in his voice.

Meredith paused, looking at her hands. Then she said, "It was, as you say, before I was born. But I find it hard to believe that our people could be enemies."

"My dear," the man said, "you are not going to find anybody to be your enemy."

She laughed at that and their foreheads almost touched as they leaned close together. Tennyson listened to a lot more of the same and then, when the two of them left the pub, he was relieved. The situation was obvious enough; the Morgan girl was one of these shy people who like to get away and play games under the protection of an assumed identity. So be it, and more power to her. Anyway, Tennyson had to hurry to get a late train back to London.

Next day, he worked all morning at his romantic comedy. Now that the group had agreed to perform the play, Tennyson was scared to death; it was simply not good enough. At half past one, he went out to his local for a pint and some food, picking up a newspaper on the way. He took a Ploughman to his favorite corner table and began enjoying the tangy cheddar cheese, pickled onion, and crusty bread and butter washed down with cool lager.

Then he saw the photograph on page three and the food went sour in his mouth. It looked a lot like the man who was buying drinks for Meredith Morgan last night. But it was the caption under the photograph that shook Tennyson—

BRIGHTON VISITOR STABBED TO DEATH

He read the story and learned the Leeds businessman had been found a few yards from the entrance to a culvert under one of the piers, dead of multiple stab wounds. Robbery was not a motive—he still had his money.

Tennyson stopped reading and stopped eating. He had to make a decision. The obvious thing to do was to go to the police. But there were unanswered questions that impeded him. First, what if the girl was not Meredith? He was ninety-eight percent sure, but that left a devilish two percent.

Worse still, what if it was her, and the man had been bush-whacked after he left her? By setting the police on her, Tennyson would be causing the girl all kinds of trouble for nothing.

For nothing? She might be able to tell the police something that would help them find the killer. That was worth a little inconvenience. Tennyson tossed that problem back and forth in his mind till three o'clock closing, by which time he was three pints further along on the day's high, but no closer to a solution on Morgan.

So he decided to visit the girl and give her a chance to explain. In German or otherwise. He left the pub and wandered on down past Ely's display windows, past the station, and on along the Broadway to the entrance to Meredith's flat. Months ago, after a rehearsal, they had dropped her here from a crowded jolly car and Meredith Morgan, typically, had ducked out with a glum goodnight.

Later that evening, over brandy at his flat, Tennyson had gotten Tony Bastable, the director, to open up about Meredith. Tony was an accountant in real life, a theatrical man only in his spare time. He was one of a type who abound in England, actors with enough talent to be only a shade or two below the Oliviers and Richardsons but who can not make it in a professional system that is grossly over-crowded. So they teach school or balance books and, making it look very easy, put on in church halls productions of a quality to stun visitors from across the Atlantic.

That night he had sat with his thin legs crossed at the ankles, his pink face wreathed in a beatific smile, sipping his brandy and talking of wartime years in India where he and a group of Air Force friends performed Shakespeare for a rajah. Then, prompted by Tennyson, he talked about Meredith Morgan.

She had been a rich girl once. She actually attended Roedean, which explained the plummy accent when she deigned to speak. Then, when she was around eighteen years old, her father managed to pull the set down around her ears.

What Mr. Morgan did was to embezzle money from his stock-broking firm in the city. The reason he stole was to meet gambling debts incurred in a casino in Grosvenor Square. One thing they frown upon in the City of London is embezzling. Not done. So Meredith's father locked himself in an air-tight room wherein he opened the gas valves without igniting a flame. Worse, he persuaded Meredith's mother to join him in this one-way ramble to eternity.

It was then that their daughter's nickname of "Merry" became permanently inappropriate. She stopped attending the prestigious private school, stopped smiling, stopped going out of the house, even stopped eating for quite a while.

It was tough going for a couple of years and, in the end, all Meredith Morgan could afford to offer the world was the cold, quiet robot so thoughtfully tolerated by the Hartfield Dramatic Society.

"Why does she go on with the acting then?" Tennyson asked.

"I suppose because she was a member before the fall," Tony said. "And today, it's her one avenue to the world."

Now, standing on the Broadway outside her door with the big red busses grumbling by and people queuing at the fruit stall in the lane, Tennyson wondered whether to ring Meredith's bell. Go ahead, he told himself. She's at work, she won't answer.

He stepped into the entrance and pressed the button. There was a click from above and the door fell ajar. Tennyson shrugged away a chilly, instinctive warning and went inside. A crumbling flight of steps led upward into a thick smell of animals and soup and rising damp. He trudged upwards, hearing a door creak open above him.

Meredith met him on the landing dressed in threadbare slacks and a sweater coated with cat hairs. A pair of ripe quilted slippers bloomed on her bare feet. "Oh, hello. Have I missed a rehearsal?"

"No. I was just walking by . There's something I have to ask you about—to settle my mind."

She drew the door almost shut behind her and stood small, the way she did onstage, with those thin arms hanging lifeless behind her back. She was not going to ask him in.

"Can we go inside?" Tennyson asked. "Just for a minute, I can't stay."

She led him in then. Tennyson was not able to look but he received an impression of twisted bedclothes, newspapers and magazines on the floor, used cotton swabs on a dresser, a mottled grey washbasin, and a pot full of something brown on top of a cooker. From the midst of all this, a heavy-eyed cat watched him with contempt.

Meredith said distantly, "I'm not well today. I couldn't go to work."

Not knowing where to begin, Tennyson said, "Where do you work?"

"The Education Authority, typing and filing. It's worth it being a civil servant; they can't sack you." Her tone of voice, the surroundings, cried out with self-pity.

Now, beyond her in a corner beside the bed, Tennyson saw the suitcase. Its shape and color, even the type of handle, identified it positively as the one he had seen in the Brighton vestibule. This made up his mind.

"Ach zo," he said thickly, "did ve haf a gut time by der zee?"

He saw no change in her but he felt a new current in the room, a slightly higher vibration. "Sorry, I didn't catch that."

"Meredith," he said, "I saw you check into that rooming house in Brighton. I heard you using a German accent, quite a good one. And I saw you pick up that man in the pub."

"What has any of that got to do with you?" It was her first speech with any fiber in it.

"Just that I saw his picture in the paper today. Somebody murdered him, Meredith. And since I know about it, and you haven't denied you were with him, I'm going to have to decide what to do with what I know."

She walked past him into the kitchen area and Tennyson had a terrible feeling she was going to offer him a cup of something. Even the thought of the utensils in this place... But she turned and said, "You'll go to the police."

"I don't want to. I don't want to make trouble for you. But that was very suspicious behavior."

"I know." She backed against the counter and turned her face in profile, and he wondered how this sad wraith had converted herself into yesterday's provocative tourist. "You know how shy I am, I can't help it. The only way I can let go is to become somebody else. That's what you saw in Brighton."

"But the murdered man. I'm right, he was your companion, wasn't he?" Her silence was enough. "So what happened? You did kill him, didn't you? I can tell."

Meredith's face crumpled and she wept like a child. Bits of explanation came through. "It was never like that before. He was cruel. He didn't want to make love, he wanted to hurt me. I had no choice. I had to defend myself."

"But he was stabbed. Do you carry a knife?"

"It was his knife. He was forcing me, on the beach by that terrible sewer. I pretended to cooperate and when he wasn't alert I grabbed the knife."

It could have been true and it could just as well not have been. But for a moment or two, Tennyson was touched by something in the girl's fierce loneliness. He remembered Tony Bastable's outline of her tragic background and saw her now as the bereaved teenager whose parents had taken the easy way out. He was not about to add to her misery.

"All right," he said, "all right, don't cry. I'm not going to the police." He found himself putting an arm around her shoulder and felt her stiffen and move away. "It's all over and done with anyway. We can't bring him back."

* * * *

So Eric Tennyson took his secret away with him and carried it through an exciting summer, during which rehearsals for his play got under way. But his imagination would not let go of the material, and he found himself working it into an outline for a drama that the society might want to stage at a later date. In the play, a shy girl from an amateur theatrical group makes regular trips to seaside resorts, assumes another character, picks up interested men, and then stabs them to death.

It was during the final week of rehearsals for his romantic comedy that Tennyson stumbled on an example of life imitating art that shook him to the ground. He was sitting alone in the dressing-room backstage at Marlborough Hall, waiting for a lighting adjustment to be made. Bored, he picked up a copy of an old newspaper left there months ago by a member of some other company using the hall. The headline on page two caught his eye.

BRIGHTON STABBING FITS PATTERN

He read on and learned that the police had linked the murder of the Leeds businessman with two others committed within the year at other resorts along the coast—Bournemouth and Ramsgate. They were working on the theory that someone connected with yachting or coastal fishing was involved.

Tennyson tore the page from the musty tabloid, folded it small, and tucked it into a pocket. He was dizzy with apprehension and guilt. He should have gone to the police right away. How would he justify himself if he called them now, months after the fact? Still, she had not been active again—if, in fact, the other cases had to do with her at all. She had admitted the first killing, in self-defense, she said. The police might be wrong in linking all three.

Tennyson was looking glumly at the floor when Tony Bastable put his ruby face through the doorway. "Come along, author. You're wanted onstage." Eric had given himself a small part in his own play, to share the praise or the blame, whichever it might be.

He followed the director up the narrow steps and was able to lose himself in the make-believe action, to put off the troublesome responsibility, at least until he could talk to Meredith Morgan again.

But she was elusive during play week, vanishing after each performance, so he decided to show her the clipping at the cast party on the Saturday following closing night. It was a triumphant week for Tennyson because the audiences loved the play. A woman with West End connections asked him for a copy of the script and said she was sending it to a chap who was always looking for comedies. Tony Bastable was ebullient and asked Tennyson what else he could give them. Eric said he had something on the fire, a thriller, and promised to show Tony an outline.

By party night, the euphoria had faded enough for Tennyson to be concerned again about the secret he was carrying. He waited for Meredith to show and when midnight arrived without her, he asked around. One of the cattier girls rolled her eyes at a friend and said, "She must have gone off on one of her trips"

"Trips?"

"Yes, didn't you know? Meredith is a loner. She saves her money and then sneaks off someplace were she can get drunk and let her hair down."

Tennyson did know. And his knowledge went further than theirs. If Meredith Morgan was about to do her thing again, he, Eric Tennyson, would be morally if not legally guilty of aiding and abetting.

He left the party and walked to Meredith's rooming house. The idea of calling the police still did not appeal to him. He was terribly late with his information and the story would be hard to follow. His best bet would be to follow the girl and head her off.

His fears were realized when she did not answer repeated rings of the bell and heavy pounding on the door. But a tiny bird of a woman did appear from another doorway on the ground floor. She was in a wheelchair and held a large cat on her lap. Tennyson knew that contemptuous look—it was Meredith's cat.

"Good evening," he said, putting on his brightest and best transatlantic voice. "I'm sorry to trouble you. I know Meredith Morgan has gone away, but she has a few pages of script in her flat and we need them for a reading. I wonder if I could just dart up and fetch them?"

"You're the lad who wrote the play."

"Yes I am."

"I didn't go. I can't go anywhere. Congratulations, I heard it was smashing."

"Well, thank you." It was a chance, so Tennyson said, "Did Meredith say where she was going this time?"

"Never. That girl comes and goes as she pleases."

"Yes. Well then, if I might have a key..."

The landlady creaked away backwards on her giant wheels. A minute later, Tennyson was on his way up the stairs. It was a blind chance; he would have to be lucky. There were no travel folders on view in the dismal room so he busied himself nosing about the telephone table. Here he saw a directory with a lot of numbers scribbled on the cover. One looked fresher than the others, and its four-digit prefix indicated it was outside London. Taking a chance, Tennyson picked up the phone and dialed the number.

After a few rings, a cheerful female voice answered and said, "Good evening, The Cliffs Hotel."

"I'm sorry to trouble you. I have a silly question. Could you tell me where you're located?"

The girl laughed. "Last time I looked, we were in Penzance."

The first train he could catch was out of Paddington Station at 9:30 in the morning. Tennyson settled himself for the six-hour trip west, down through Devon and into Cornwall. He knew he was being shown some of the most beautiful countryside in the world but his mind would not let him enjoy it. He had to find Meredith Morgan fast. And then he had to decide what to do with her.

Penzance, the end of the line, came up a little after half past three. A stretch of sea on the left dazzled Tennyson—it was an indescribable blue and there was so much water he felt dizzy and had to grasp the rough train seat. There was no end to it—the sea was freedom, the sea pulled you away from the land.

The Cliffs Hotel was only a five-minute walk from the station. Tennyson went and stood outside, not knowing what to do. Meredith would not be registered under her own name. Would she be pretending again to be German? Perhaps, but not necessarily. Even so, how could he inquire without a name?

He began to feel the pressure of time. She would probably not be in her room on a sunny Sunday afternoon. But supposing she followed her Brighton pattern and chose a pub—Penzance had pubs on every corner.

Tennyson turned from the hotel and started walking. After all, Meredith was a visitor too. She could only have drifted down this hill and onto the main street, working up the other hill past the station. And he was in luck with English pub hours; they were all closed till six so she had to be circulating.

It was almost six o'clock when he saw her. She was standing with a man outside a pub called The Turk's Head, the red plastic bag hanging over her shoulder, her hip cocked in a coquettish pose. The man was portly, his face florid in a frame of curly grey hair.

As Tennyson watched, the pub door was opened from the inside and the couple went through, ducking their heads under the low lintel. Not wanting to waste a second, Tennyson hurried across the street and stepped down into the entry. There were two doors, the Saloon Bar and The Snug. He tried the latter and found Meredith sitting alone on an upholstered bench. Her eyes widened.

"Where's your friend?" he said.

"In the loo."

"Good." He produced the newspaper story and showed it to her. She only glanced at it. "You admitted the Brighton killing and here are the police saying it's one of a set. How do you explain that?"

The portly man was back. Meredith spoke first, her German accent sounding impeccable. "I'm sorry, I lied to you. I am not alone. This is my husband, he has found me, and I am a bad girl."

Portly gave a gallant bow. "You could never be a bad girl, my dear. Sir, you are a lucky man." He insisted on buying them drinks and departed, wishing them years of happiness, hinting they needed babies to turn their marriage to gold like his.

Alone now, Meredith lowered her voice and dropped the accent. She admitted the crimes and said, through tears, that she could not help herself. Leaning close to Tennyson, taking his arm, she was everything the Meredith back in Wimbledon was not. He found himself feeling very sorry for her while an inner voice told him they were in this together—which, after his months of silence, was true enough.

"Look," he said during a second round of drinks, "we don't have to be Freudians to see the problems you've had to cope with. I heard about your parents' suicide and how that turned your life around."

"My life was miserable before that. They never loved me. They only loved each other. Oh, they gave me clothes and money and private schools. But that was to shut me up and keep me out of their sight." Her voice was flat.

Tapping the message out with a fingertip on the back of her hand, Tennyson said, "It can still be all right. You've got your whole life ahead of you. I know you're broke now but we can get you into some sort of psychotherapy on the National Health. Or I can pay for a specialist—I've got money. No, listen to me. You can talk out this hostility and not have to go after older men."

"But after what I've done..."

"I've never believed in punishment for its own sake. Those men can't be brought back to life. The thing is to salvage your life."

He spent the night with her in her room at The Cliffs. A wind blew up and brought rain to lash the bay window, and beyond that sound breakers pulsed and crashed against the shingle beach. On an impulse, he asked her to speak to him in her German accent. She did, crooning romantic syllables in a husky voice, and he was overcome with desire for this strange, dangerous woman.

In the morning, the sky was blue again, the sea choppy under a brisk wind. Their best train to London was at four o'clock so they were left with hours to kill.

Meredith said, "Let's take a bus to Land's End. As long as we're here, it's a shame not to see it."

So they boarded a green coach and drove along winding country roads, the drystone walls ablaze with gorse in golden bloom. At Land's End, the wind was fierce and the mass of tourists headed for the safety of the hotel with its bars and lounges.

"Can we survive this hurricane?" Tennyson said, holding Meredith by both arms, finding it difficult to catch his breath.

"Don't be a coward," she said.

They walked round the hotel and crossed a dry decline to where an outcropping of eroded rock marked the southwestern tip of England. A white signpost indicated mileages to places like John O'Groats. The wind was incredible—Tennyson had never experienced anything like it. It was more than a movement of air; it had substance, as if they were standing in the rush of an avalanche.

"A little of this goes a long way!" he shouted.

Meredith was looking around. "We're the only brave ones," she said. "I love it." She moved from his side and ventured across a sloping rock, sitting down on it, bracing her feet, then peering over at the sea. She looked back over her shoulder and he was struck by her childlike beauty. With her hair streaming flat across her cheek, she looked twelve years old.

"Come and see the color of the water!" she shouted. "It's unbelievable!"

He crept over the rock and edged to a position beside her. She was right, the water below was churned to an electric foam, boiling and reaching upward with sheets of spray.

Then her foot was kicking at his and her hand was in the small of his back and he felt himself sliding forward over the edge. In that last moment, he saw her eyes and noted that they were intent, filled with a fierce determination. And he thought of his success, of all the plays he was going to write, and there ought to be something he could do but he was head down now and screaming as he fell.

Tony Bastable was astonished and saddened by the tragedy at Land's End. Imagine old Eric being involved with Meredith like that. The American had never said anything; he didn't even seem to like the girl particularly. A faint whisper of suspicion sounded in Bastable's mind but he could not link it with anything.

As for Meredith, she had been a sad enough figure up till now. How could they possibly cope with her after this?

However, life must go on. More particularly, the life of the Hartfield Dramatic Society. Pity they had found a local playwright only to lose him after one success. Still, Tennyson had offered them his new play, so Bastable felt no qualms in rescuing it from his flat.

If the outline had merit, another writer could develop it and they would have a nice newsy production, a posthumous premiere!

He settled into his armchair, stretched his legs, and began to read. Then Tony Bastable's intelligent eyes began to widen perceptively as he learned about the unloved actress who travelled to seaside resorts and killed strangers, and who was found out by a writer who pursued her, which left her with no choice but to kill him.

Enter the lively and lurid world
of DIME CRIME!

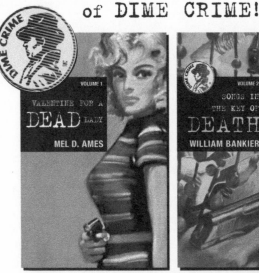

Dime Crime is an exciting new series collecting some of the best crime short stories by many of the legendary and overlooked authors in the genre. To learn more about past and future volumes in the series, or details about the authors and their stories, visit the Dime Crime website for details:

www.dimecrime.com